MW01135158

MURDER IN THE PAINTED LADY

A PEYTON BROOKS' MYSTERY

VOLUME 0

ML Hamilton

authormlhamilton.net

Cover by Kyler Lugo

MURDER IN THE PAINTED LADY

© 2017 ML Hamilton, Sacramento, CA

All rights reserved. No part of this book may be reproduced or transmitted in any form or by any means without written permission from the author, except by a reviewer who may quote brief passages in a review to be printed by a newspaper, magazine or journal.

First print

All Characters appearing in this work are fictitious. Any resemblance to real persons, living or dead, is purely coincidental.

This book is dedicated to the fans who remain loyal throughout every change. You are appreciated.

It is easier to build strong children than to repair broken men.

~ Frederick Douglass

CHAPTER 1

Hey, Darla, it's Jules. I just wanted to tell you I got the listing on Mason. Seven mil, baby. Don't be too jealous. You've got your Painted Lady and all. Let's get together for drinks to celebrate. We're gonna be millionaires! I see Mercedes in our futures. Call me so we can coordinate our schedules. I got a showing at 2:00 and then I need to put in a few hours at the office, but I should be done by 6:00 at the latest. I can pick you up or we can meet at the bar. It's your turn to pick the place. Talk to you soon, girl. Bye.

* * *

Lori walked up the steps before her clients, a young couple that had met at Google and married a year later. She loved this new crop of clients, high paying jobs and only a few years out of college. Of course, it was pushing home prices in San Francisco beyond anything people had ever seen, but she had no problem reaping the reward. Her new clients were book smart and money flush, without a lot of life experience.

When they told her they wanted to own a unique bit of San Francisco, this house had come to mind. One of the famed painted ladies, it had yellow siding, white trim and accents of brick red. She typed in her code to unlock the box on the front door handle and pushed it open, giving them their first view of the interior.

They were such a cute couple. The young woman grabbed her husband's hand and let out a little squeal of delight. He beamed down at her. Lori was having a hard time remembering their names. She removed her business card from her pocket and looked at the back where she'd scribbled them down.

Darcy and Ethan Cox.

"Come inside," Lori said, motioning them into the interior.

The entrance opened on a long hall with dark, polished wood floors and white wainscoting. The walls were painted a soft butter yellow above the wainscoting.

"The floors are all original as is most of the woodwork."

The Coxs murmured in wonder. She led them into the sunlit living room with its tray ceiling painted a darker color than the walls and the bay windows overlooking the park. From there they entered the semi-circular breakfast nook with windows on three of the four sides and its newly tiled floors. The kitchen had been recently remodeled, the stainless steel appliances gleaming in the sunlight streaming through the open windows.

"The kitchen has gourmet appliances, top of the line."

"Oh, we don't cook," said Darcy, clinging to her husband's arm. "But it's pretty."

Lori nodded. Of course they didn't cook. Who had time to cook when you were making millions? "As you know, San Francisco's famous for its restaurants."

They giggled at that.

"Can you show us the bedrooms?" asked Ethan and he gave Darcy a lecherous look. She swatted at him, hiding her face against his shoulder.

Lori tried not to throw up a little. *Remember the money,* she told herself.

"This way." She stepped around them, leading the way to the stairs. They climbed to the second floor and Lori showed them the five bedrooms, all in a row, and the two bathrooms. Of course, they complained there wasn't a bathroom in the master bedroom.

"This house was built in 1892. They didn't have en suite bedrooms then."

"1892," said Ethan in awe, staring up at the tray ceiling in the master bedroom. "Can you believe that?" he asked Darcy.

"And it could be ours," she said, her eyes gleaming.

Let it be theirs, let it be theirs, prayed Lori. With this commission, even splitting it with the listing agent, she'd be able to pay off her daughter's school loans, buy a new car, and sock some away in the bank in case there was another real estate downturn. "Well, what do you think? Should we go downstairs and write up an offer?"

The Coxs looked at each other, silently communicating. Then Darcy nodded and Lori had to resist rubbing her hands together in anticipation.

Ethan smiled at Lori. "Before we do that, I'd like to see the garage."

"The garage?" Lori tried to hide her disappointment. She was hoping to write up the offer as quickly as she could, get it sent over to the listing agent, then jet off for a massage and a pedicure before going home. Who gave a damn about garages in San Francisco? "It's the typical garage. One car, accessed at street level."

"I still want to see it. I like to work on vintage cars and I want to make sure there's enough room for my 67' Mustang."

"Wow! That must be quite the car."

"It's gorgeous," said Darcy.

Lori couldn't care less about cars. They were a tool to get you from Point A to Point B. She drove an Acura, but mainly because you had to project prosperity to get prosperity, but it meant little else to her. She forced a smile. "Let's go see the garage."

She led them to the stairs and they descended. Her feet were starting to hurt in these damn heels and she didn't want to walk down another flight of stairs below this one, except she wasn't letting these two out of her sight until she had a deal on the table. She wasn't foolish enough to give them time to talk amongst themselves without her listening in. She'd been burned like that before.

The door to the garage had been snuck into a corner of the kitchen. She unlocked it and pulled it open, reaching in to turn on the light. The staircase down was steep, but she gripped the handrail and preceded them into the dank, shadowy room. It smelled of mildew and something else she couldn't identify. When they got to the bottom of the stairs, she searched for another light switch.

She'd toured this property when they'd had the realtors' walk-through, but she hadn't come down to the garage. She turned a circle on the landing and finally located the switch next to a juncture box for the electricity. Flipping it on, she shifted to step down onto the garage floor, but Darcy suddenly let out a blood curdling scream.

Lori's eyes snapped up to the open area. A body lay sprawled in the middle of the concrete floor, brown hair fanned out in a halo around her head. She wore a navy blue pantsuit and heels, her hands folded on her breast. Lori couldn't move, just stood, gripping the railing, while Darcy continued to scream.

* * *

Lori picked up her cell phone and looked at the time. She sat at the table in the breakfast nook with Darcy and Ethan huddled together at the other end. Cops swarmed the Victorian, snapping pictures, measuring things, laying down markers. More than an hour had passed and beyond a cursory few questions, no one had asked them anything else. She wondered how long they were going to be kept here. She just wanted to go home, she wanted a shower, and she wanted to drink enough that she'd forget what she'd seen.

She knew the woman in the garage. They'd never talked much, but they'd worked on a number of deals together. Darla Stevens had to be Lori's age, maybe a year or two younger. She'd been a realtor in San Francisco for the

4

last ten years or so. She was pretty, likeable, and professional. If she told you she was going to do something, she always came through. Lori had liked that about her.

After they'd found her, Ethan had worked up the courage to go up to the body. He'd felt for a pulse, but it was pretty obvious she was dead. She had bruises all around her neck where someone had strangled her.

Lori shivered now. It was the very thing her husband had always feared, that one time she'd go into a house and someone would either rape her or kill her. He'd wanted her to quit for years now, but the money was too good. They had three kids to get through college and already they'd gone into debt for Lauren.

She glanced up as a young African American woman stepped into the breakfast nook. She couldn't have topped five foot four, her hair pulled up in a ponytail. She wore a leather jacket and combat boots with jeans. She had a pretty enough face, but her eyes were gorgeous. Large, dark, and heavily lashed, they gave her entire appearance an exotic look.

She pulled back the side of her leather jacket and unhooked the badge from her belt, showing it to Lori, then flashing it at the Coxs. "I'm Inspector Peyton Brooks," she said.

Lori held out her hand. "Lori Hardy."

The inspector shook it, then walked around the table and shook hands with the Coxs.

"Ethan and Darcy Cox," said Ethan.

Inspector Brooks took a small notebook out of her pocket and wrote something on it. Lori eyed her more closely. She couldn't even be twenty-five. How the hell was she an inspector?

"Brooks?" came a deep male voice.

Brooks turned and looked toward the kitchen doorway. "In here," she said.

A moment later, the doorway filled with the handsomest man Lori had ever seen. He too couldn't have been more than twenty-five, if that. He towered at least a foot over Brooks with black hair that touched his broad shoulders and blue eyes. His features had the symmetry of a male model and he had the build of an athlete.

Lori let out a breath in appreciation.

"Bob thinks you should see the body."

Brooks made a face. "I thought I'd take a statement from the witnesses first."

The man gave her a stern look. "Brooks."

She held up a hand. "Tell Bob I'll be there in a minute."

"Fine," he said and disappeared again.

Peyton offered Lori a self-deprecating smile. "That's my partner, Inspector D'Angelo," she said, coming the table and pulling out a chair. She sank into it.

"Inspector," said Lori, clasping her hands on the tabletop, "how much longer do we have to wait here?"

"Just a little longer. I need to take your statements, get your contact information, then you can leave." She set the notebook on the table. "Did you know the victim?"

Lori tried not to think of the body, but it was all she could see. "Yes, she's Darla Stevens, a fellow realtor. She works for Bay Cities Properties."

Brooks wrote in her notebook. "Did you know her well?"

Lori shook her head. "I knew her professionally. I don't think we ever exchanged personal information."

Brooks nodded and wrote some more. "What were you doing in the house?"

Lori glanced at the Coxs and it suddenly hit her, they would never buy this house now. She'd just lost the biggest commission of her life, damn it. "I was showing the Coxs the house. They were interested in buying a Painted Lady."

"Okay. When you found the body, what did you do?"

Lori frowned. "What?"

"What did you do? I need to know everyone's actions from the moment the body was found."

"I screamed," said Darcy. "Lori turned on the light and I saw her and I just started screaming. I couldn't stop."

"Okay, what about you?" Brooks asked Lori.

"I just stared at her for a moment, trying to let it sink in." She shivered. Dear God, they'd found a body. The thought kept ambushing her. "Then I called 911."

"And Mr. Cox?" asked Brooks.

"I went down to see if she was alive."

"Did you touch her?"

"I felt for a pulse. I didn't do anything else."

Brooks wrote.

"Is that okay? I mean, I had to see if she was still alive. I didn't mean to mess up any evidence or anything. I just wanted to see if she was alive."

Brooks regarded him without speaking for a moment, then she scribbled something on her pad. Turning back to Lori, she said, "Did you expect Darla to be in the house when you showed it?"

"No. I called her and told her I had interested clients. She told me to bring them over." Lori turned in her seat and pointed to the door. "There's a lockbox on the front door for us to use."

"So you had no idea Darla might be here?"

"None. In fact, she said she had another appointment across town."

"Did she say who it was with?"

Lori shook her head. "We weren't close like that. We were just colleagues."

A uniformed officer appeared in the doorway. He had a thick moustache and a thatch of dark hair. "Hey, Brooks, D'Angelo wants you to come down and look at the body. They're ready to transport."

Brooks sighed. "Got it, Frank. Tell D'Angelo I'm on my way."

"Are you, though?"

She shifted in the chair and glared at him.

The officer gave her a closed-mouth smile, but she didn't return it. With a chuckle, he walked away again.

"Can you give me your contact information?" Brooks said, flipping to a clean page and sliding the notebook to the Coxs. "Just in case I have more questions."

Ethan took the notebook and pen, scribbling on the pad.

Lori shifted uncomfortably. "Inspector Brooks?"

The dark eyes swung to her. "Yes?"

Lori tried to formulate what she wanted to ask, but it seemed so calloused to be worrying about herself at this moment.

Brooks reached over and covered Lori's hands with her own. "I think this is an isolated incident," she said. "I don't think you have anything to worry about."

Lori nodded, glad the inspector had anticipated her question without her having to ask.

"Although," she said, patting her hand. "It wouldn't hurt to carry mace or pepper spray, now would it?"

Lori shook her head. Her husband had wanted her to carry a taser, but she'd scoffed at him. She wasn't scoffing now.

Brooks took a business card out of her pocket and passed it to Lori. "If you think of anything or remember something about Darla, please call me."

Lori picked up the card, studying it. Brooks couldn't be more than a year or two older than her own daughter, Lauren. What the hell did she know about solving murders? But she put the card in her pocket just the same, feeling better for having it.

*   *   *

Peyton made her way down the steep staircase to the garage. She couldn't deny this Painted Lady impressed her. Built in the late 19th century, the old girl had held up against the relentless march of time. It was sure a lot nicer than the little house on 19th that she was renting...well, about to own.

The money from her father's insurance policy had come through and the owners of her little shack were willing to deal. Peyton wasn't certain how she felt about owning property. It seemed like a really grown-up thing to do, but she knew it would have made her father happy.

Her thoughts scattered as she hesitated on the landing. Marco had begun climbing toward her and he gave her a stern look. "Did you finally decide to stop chitchatting with the bubblegum millionaires?"

"Bubblegum millionaires?" she said, frowning.

He gripped the railing on either side in his hands, his shoulders straining the ribbed sweater he wore. His gun peeked out beneath his arm. "You know, the Google tech geniuses that are driving housing prices through the roof. Because of them, I can only eat twice a week since rent just keeps climbing."

She gave him a sultry look. "You could always move in with me, Marco baby."

He shook his head and straightened. "Hell no. I ain't one of your charity cases, Brooks. So, you think you wanna do your job now?"

"You mean look at a dead body?"

"That's exactly what I mean."

"Haven't you done enough looking for the both of us?"

"Bob wanted you to see it. I don't know, he thinks you've got good instincts or something."

She elbowed her way past him, *accidentally* hitting him in the stomach. He made an oof sound and pretended to double over. Uniforms blocked her initial view of the body, standing in a cluster, talking to each other.

"You getting enough of a thrill, gentlemen?" she said.

Drew Holmes turned and gave her a bored look. He kept his hair so close cropped, his pink scalp showed through, and he had a hooked nose. He wasn't her favorite uniform. Frank Smith looked contrite, stepping out of the way. A few uniforms from another precinct wandered off, giving Holmes and Smith commiserate shakes of their heads.

The body lay behind Holmes, sprawled on her back, her arms folded on her chest. She was in her late thirties, early forties, pretty with dark brown hair. Peyton swallowed hard. The smell of death was heavy in the room, along with a hint of mildew. She didn't want to get any closer, but Bob Anderson looked up at her.

"You wanna come a little closer?" he said.

Her eyes cut to Holmes and he gave a little smile. She didn't want to get any closer, but damned if she was going to let Holmes have the satisfaction of busting her chops about it. Marco exited the stairwell, talking into his cell phone. By the sound of his voice, she knew he was calling for the coroner's bus to pick up their victim.

Once he was at her back, she lifted her chin and walked toward Holmes, forcing him to step away. Years ago she'd decided she would never back down to that rat bastard. Of course, having six foot four Marco behind her helped.

She focused her attention on Bob's perpetual five o'clock shadow. "Her name's Darla Stevens," she said.

"You get that from the bubblegum millionaires?" asked Marco.

"I got that from the bubblegum millionaires' realtor."

Marco gave a grunt.

Bob squatted beside the body, wearing gloves, his camera resting on the concrete floor beside him. "I think she's been dead more than 24 hours. Rigor's come and gone."

Peyton nodded, still not looking at the body. "It doesn't look like she was sexually assaulted." The glimpse Peyton had gotten revealed she wore a conservative navy blue pantsuit.

"No, it doesn't look like sexual assault, although the way the body's arranged seems almost...I don't know," said Bob, exhaling in frustration.

Peyton forced herself to look down. Darla Stevens had been arranged, her suit straightened, her hands folded primly on her chest, her legs together, and her feet in their expensive pumps ankle to ankle. Her hair had been fanned out around her head like a halo.

"Where's her purse?"

Bob shrugged. "I didn't find one."

"What about car keys?"

"Nope."

Peyton glanced at Marco. "Is there a car outside? Can we get some uniforms checking the ones on the street?"

Marco nodded and motioned to Holmes and Smith. They headed toward the stairs.

Bob brushed the back of his gloved hand over his prominent widow's peak. "This is what I don't get." He pointed to her neck.

Peyton forced herself to hunker down opposite Bob and stare at the ligature marks on her neck. "Did you lift her head?"

"Yep."

"Any fingerprints on the back of her neck?"

"No fingerprints, but the ligature marks extend all the way around."

"How'd he strangle her then?" asked Marco, looming at Peyton's back.

"I can't figure it out. I had the uniforms search the whole garage for a murder weapon, but I don't know what it is. It's not rope. That would have left thread marks or burns. It's not a garrote because that would have cut into her skin, and it wasn't with his hands."

Peyton gave Bob a surprised look. Honestly, he didn't know what she'd been strangled with?

"What?" he protested.

Bob wasn't the smartest cookie, but when she looked up at Marco, his face looked just as blank. "You don't know what he could have strangled her with?"

Bob huffed in exasperation. "That's why I wanted you to come down."

"She was strangled with a scarf."

Their faces still appeared blank.

Peyton motioned to her own neck, but she didn't often wear something so froufrou to work. "A silk scarf."

Bob's face lit with recognition. "Where is it?"

Peyton had a sinking feeling in the pit of her stomach. She figured she knew where the scarf was and why he wanted it. He was keeping souvenirs.

CHAPTER 2

Darla, this is Gerald! What the hell! I told you I wanted to come by today and pick up my cufflinks. You said I could. You promised to meet me at the house at 4:30. What gives? If you weren't going to let me have the cufflinks, you should have said so. I'm getting really sick of your irresponsibility. Damn it, just do what you promised to do!

*   *   *

Peyton and Marco drove back to the precinct after the coroner's bus took Darla Stevens away. Climbing out of the Charger, Marco's pride and joy, he waited for her to get out, then he pressed the lock.

"Call Abe and see if he can get the body," he said as she fell into step beside him.

Peyton pulled out her phone and dialed the medical examiner's cell phone. He picked up on the third ring.

"Hey, little soul sister, you wanna meet for drinks tonight?"

"Can't," she said, imagining the flamboyant ME with his wild dreadlocks and brilliant smile. She could just imagine what he might be wearing – whatever it was, it would be loud and unique, just as he was himself. She felt a little disappointed that they couldn't meet him for drinks, but there was no way they'd be finished in time. "We have a case. Can you see if you can get the body for an autopsy?"

"Hold on, sweets, let me grab a pen and paper."

Peyton and Marco climbed the stairs outside the precinct and Marco held the door open for her to pass through before him. He was always thoughtful that way. She pushed the half-door with her hip, Marco on her heels. Glancing to her right, she saw that Captain Defino's office door was closed. Maria's desk was empty, but a moment later she appeared from the back, carrying a piece of chocolate cake with what looked like raspberry filling.

Peyton's eyes zeroed in on it. "Where'd that come from?"

Maria looked as if she smelt something bad, taking a large bite of the cake. "The break room. Geez, Brooks, where else would I get it? The bathroom?"

Peyton started to answer, but Abe was back on the line.

"Okay, sugar lips, shoot me the name," he said.

"Darla Stevens," Peyton said.

"Spell it."

So Peyton did.

"Can Bob send me whatever pictures he took and a list of the evidence he collected at the scene?" asked Abe.

"I'll tell him."

"Can he send it to my correct email? Last time, I think he sent it to Mongolia, because I surely did not get it."

Peyton sighed. Bob Anderson wasn't the most responsible, conscientious CSI they'd ever had. It made her miss Chuck Wilson, who'd retired a few years ago. Now there was a man's man, a tough old bastard, but he always dotted his i's and crossed his t's.

Peyton covered the receiver part of her cell phone. "Is there any cake left?" she asked Maria, watching her place another bite in her mouth.

Marco shook his head and pushed past her, going toward their desks.

"As if you need cake, Brooks," said Maria. "You ain't never getting a man if your trunk's as big as a...well, trunk."

Peyton gave her an arch look as Abe laughed in her ear.

"That Maria is such a saucy wench," he said.

"If my trunk is as big as a trunk? Seriously? Not one of your better insults."

"My blood sugar's low," said Maria, looking away.

"It won't be in a minute," said Peyton, headed to the back. "Just send me a text, Abe, when you find out if you can pull our case."

"Anything for you, sweets. So tell me, what's my Angel'D wearing today?"

Peyton paused by Marco's desk. He was sipping a mug of coffee. She turned dramatically to look at her own desk. No cake. "Did you not hear me say I wanted cake?"

"I heard."

"But you didn't think to get me some when you went into the break room?"

"I figured you could use the exercise."

Peyton drew a deep breath and released it. "What's Marco wearing today, Abe?" she said.

Marco's eyes widened and he waved his hands to stop her.

"Hot pink bikini briefs and a see-through muscle shirt."

"Oh my," said Abe and she could almost see him fanning himself.

She smiled wickedly at her partner.

He smiled back at her.

"I've got to go," said Abe breathlessly, "something's on fire."

"I'll bet," she said, laughing.

"Talk to you soon, sugar lips."

"Talk to you soon, Abe." She disconnected the call.

"You're evil, Brooks, you know that?"

She leaned over him. "You have no idea," she said, then walked into the break room after her cake.

* * *

Tapping her foot impatiently, she watched Bob Anderson rifle through the mess in his cubicle, looking for the notes he'd taken on the case. His camera sat on the edge of the desk balanced precariously and his evidence kit was open, evidence bags, disposable gloves, and vials shoved inside in a haphazard mess.

"You need to get organized."

"Don't keep at me, Brooks. I'm doing the best I can."

"There isn't evidence from another case in there, is there?" she said, pointing at the label on an evidence bag.

He glanced at it. "That's just a cigarette butt from Cho and Simons' BART station jumper."

"Why isn't it at the lab being analyzed?"

Bob looked at her, a muscle in his jaw twitching. "He jumped in front of a BART train, Brooks. He didn't die of lung cancer."

"But you collected it for a reason," she said.

"Cho told me to. He wanted it tested for illegal substances."

Peyton held out her hands, her eyes going wide with disbelief. "Seriously, Anderson, are you stupid?"

"You know what!" said Bob, jumping to his feet.

Before she could react, Marco was suddenly between them, a heavy hand on Bob's shoulder, shoving him back into his seat. "Let's just take a breath, okay?" he told Bob.

"She's always picking on me!"

"Just take a deep breath," Marco said again, then he turned and moved into Peyton's personal space, forcing her to take a step back herself. "Let me handle this."

"He has evidence in his case from Cho and Simons' jumper. That should have been at the lab yesterday." She pointed to the evidence.

"Brooks," said Marco firmly. "Go see if Stan can get anything off her cell phone." He handed her a slip of paper. "I got the number from the real estate agent who found her body."

Peyton frowned, looking at the number. When had he talked to Lori? As far as she knew, she'd been the only one to question her. Of course, Lori was a woman and Marco had a way with women. She was surprised he didn't have Lori's personal number too, then she decided she didn't want to know if he did.

"Fine." She looked past his shoulder at Bob, who had his head braced on his hand. "Get that evidence to the lab!" she ordered, pointing at him.

Bob slammed his hand down on the desk, scattering papers and rattling the camera. As they watched in horror, the camera tilted and started to fall.

Marco snatched it by the strap at the last minute.

They all breathed out a sigh of relief.

Peyton backpedaled quickly, hurrying around the corner of Bob's cubicle, headed toward the supply closet Stan had made into an office.

Stan Neumann was the precinct's tech genius. A small, mousy man with curly brown hair and coke-bottle glasses, who wore t-shirts with silly sayings on them, he was probably the smartest man Peyton knew, next to Abe. He was also one of the sweetest.

He'd taken a supply closet and filled it with electronic equipment. He had a massive desktop with three monitors and a laptop, and sometimes a tablet. On the wall directly opposite the door, he'd hung shelves and those shelves were choked with dolls. *Action figures,* Peyton mentally corrected herself. Whenever she called them dolls, he got mildly offended. She didn't like to offend Stan. The action figures were all in their original boxes because he told her they were worth more that way.

He'd placed a table over the door, so no one could just come inside and mess with his equipment. Not that anyone would. It looked like ground control in here and Peyton always felt anxious when she visited. As soon as she stepped up to the door, he wheeled around to face her and his face lit up.

"Peyton, hey, how are you?"

"Good, Stan, and you?"

"I'm hunky dory." His eyes swept down her body, not in a lecherous way, but appreciative. "I like the leather jacket.

You look all badass." He widened his eyes until they appeared enormous behind his glasses.

"Thanks," she said with a laugh and held out the slip of paper. "Can you get a warrant to search this woman's phone? I need any information you can find out about her."

"I'll get right on it."

"If you can get me her address too, that would help."

"What happened to her purse?"

Peyton leaned against the doorjamb. "We couldn't find it. We didn't find a car at the scene or anything personal on her body."

"Yowsa," he said.

Peyton nodded. "We wouldn't even have a name if the person who found her hadn't known who she was."

"I guess you want a license plate number on the car if there is one, so you can put out an APB?"

"That'd be awesome, Stan."

He beamed at her. "Can I call you if I get any information?"

"You know you can."

He looked down, his fingers folding the message into a tiny square. "Hey, Peyton?"

She gave him a fond lift of her brows.

"I was wondering…"

"Brooks!" came Marco's bellow.

She looked down the hallway toward the main room, then she turned back to Stan. She hated it when Marco bellowed at her. "What, Stan?"

"I was wondering if…"

"Brooks!"

She winced. "I'll be there in a minute. Stop shouting at me!"

"Defino wants an update."

"Go. I'll be right behind you!" She turned back to Stan and forced a smile.

He looked like a rabbit that wanted to bolt.

"You were wondering if…"

He shook his head. "It's nothing. Forget it."

She exhaled, trying to keep her composure. This is what you got when you worked in a predominately male profession. "Okay. Well, if you decide differently, you can text me." She started to turn away.

"...if you'd go on a date with me."

Peyton stopped moving, her back to Stan's doorway. She wasn't sure she'd heard him right. Slowly she turned to face him, giving him a quizzical look.

He gave a hysterical laugh. "That's ridiculous, right? Yeah, that's ridiculous."

"Stan."

"No, no, it's okay." He held up a hand. "Forget it. I know a woman like you would NEVER be seen with a guy like me."

Damn it all. She rubbed her hand across her forehead. "Stan."

"The guys online, they said you gotta take a risk. I mean, I can go into battle against the Orc hoard, but I can't ask a woman out on a date. It's really ridiculous, but I mean look at you and look at me."

"I'll go!"

Stan stopped talking and blinked at her owlishly. "What?"

"I'll go. I'll go on a date with you."

"Really?"

"Really."

"Tomorrow night?"

Wow, he moved fast. "Sure. Tomorrow night."

"Can I pick you up at your house?"

"Sure. I'll text you the address."

He waved that off. "I'll just get it off..." Then he faltered as he saw the alarmed look on Peyton's face. He must have realized he sounded a little stalkerish. "Text me your address. Is 7:00 okay?"

If you were in high school, but she forced a smile, already wondering if she hadn't made a mistake. Oh God, when Marco found out or Holmes, oh God, when Holmes found out, she would never live it down.

What? You gonna get matching Star Trek uniforms? He can be Captain Kirk and you can be Lieutenant Uhura. Kinky.

Stan was saying something, so she shook herself out of her musings.

"What?"

"I was just saying we probably shouldn't let anyone know. They might think it's a conflict of interest or something."

She snatched that up, pointing at him. "Good idea, Stan. Besides, we'll just keep it our little secret."

She hadn't meant to go all sultry on him, but she heard the way it came out, especially when his mouth dropped open and his eyes got even wider. He gave her a goofy smile.

"Right, our secret," he said breathlessly.

Oh God, this was such a bad idea. Such a bad, bad idea. Defino was going to kill her if she found out.

"See you tomorrow night," she said, backing away.

He leaned forward, his head peeking out of his closet. "Tomorrow night," he called after her.

She quickened her pace and turned the corner, almost smashing into Drew Holmes as he headed for the back of the precinct. He gave her a lazy smile.

"What about tomorrow night, Brooks?" he said, waggling his brows.

Peyton tilted up her chin. "Tomorrow night I get the knowledge that for a few beautiful hours, Holmes, I can forget your ugly mug."

He gave her a jerk of his chin. "All righty, then. All righty." And he walked around her.

Glancing to her left, she saw Bob Anderson glaring at her, his head braced on his hand again. She glared back at him, then she headed to the front of the precinct to meet Marco.

*   *   *

Katherine Defino was of medium height with brown hair cut into a stylish bob and brown eyes that always squinted. She needed glasses or contacts or something, but she refused, declaring staunchly that she didn't need any eye assistance. Peyton wasn't sure of the reason for the rebellion – seeing seemed like a pretty good reason to get glasses – but Defino was determined.

Her office was always dark, the blinds drawn and the lights turned down low. She had a glass topped desk, shelves holding binders of legal precedence, and two ultra modern, white melamine chairs. Peyton hated those chairs. They didn't conform to any sort of human body and she always felt like she was in danger of sliding off onto the floor.

Marco already occupied the chair closest to the door, his long legs stretched out before him, his hands folded on his flat belly. He gave her a lazy smirk as she angled around behind him and slid into the other chair. It would be so much easier if he just took the chair further into the room, but Marco loved to goad her whenever he could.

Captain Defino was reading something on her computer, her eyes squinting. She glanced over as Peyton fussed, trying to get comfortable in the unforgiving chair. "Why are you fighting with Bob Anderson?" Defino asked.

Peyton slapped Marco in the chest with the back of her hand. The smirk continued as he lifted his hand and rubbed the spot.

"Brooks, you need to learn to play well with others," scolded Defino.

"Then others should do their jobs." She pointed out the door. "He's got evidence in his case, Captain, evidence that should have been turned over to the lab yesterday."

"I'm aware of that, but you still don't play well with others, Brooks. What am I supposed to do if no one wants to work with you?"

21

Peyton lowered her head, chastised. "Okay, okay. I'll back off a little."

Defino and Marco exchanged amused looks. "Tell me about the case. Who's our vic?"

"Darla Stevens," said Peyton, taking out her notebook. "She was a real estate agent who had a listing for a Painted Lady on Postcard Row. That's all I've got so far. I need to run her license and see if she was married, what her home address was. Stan's pulling a warrant to get her cell phone records and the license plate number on her car."

"Did you find her car?"

Marco and Peyton both shook their heads, then Peyton continued, "Her purse was missing and we didn't find a car. She might not even have one."

"The people who found her? What about them?"

"One is a realtor herself, Lori Hardy, and the two others were Hardy's clients, Darcy and Ethan Cox. They're just a couple of..." She gave Marco a mischievous look. "What did you call them again?"

He gave her a shake of his head, fighting a smile.

"Oh, right, bubblegum millionaires."

"What?" asked Defino.

"You know, Google wunderkind." She braced her hands on either side of the chair and shifted again.

"Okay. Get a warrant to pull her driver's license record and find an address. We need to notify next of kin."

"On it," said Peyton, starting to rise, but a knock at the door stopped her.

Maria poked her head inside. "Captain, the new ADA is here to talk with you?"

"Send him in," said Defino, motioning with her hand. "You need to meet him," she told her two detectives.

Peyton settled back in the seat and looked over as the door opened wider. A tall, African American man stepped through, his white teeth flashing in a brilliant smile. He wore a perfectly tailored suit and had short cropped black hair. While he might not be as gorgeous as her partner, this guy had classical good looks – strong nose, wide-set dark eyes, and a square jaw. He also smelled wonderful, like fresh linens dried on a line.

Peyton sucked in a breath of admiration, drawing a scowl from Marco. She didn't care. This guy was sexy.

The man shifted the smile to her, then stepped between her and Marco, extending his hand to Defino. "Captain, I'm Devan Adams, the new ADA."

Defino rose and took his hand. "Mr. Adams, it is a pleasure to meet you." She released him and motioned to Peyton and Marco. "This is one of my finest detective teams, Inspector Peyton Brooks and Inspector Marco D'Angelo."

Peyton rose and gave him her hand. He beamed at her, making her stomach do a little flutter, then he covered her hand with his free one. "Inspector Brooks," he said, his voice warm like melted chocolate. "Pleasure to meet you."

"Same," she said, smiling back at him. Oh goodness, he smelled even better up close.

He released her and turned to Marco. "Inspector D'Angelo."

Marco didn't bother to get up. He gave him a firm handshake. "DA," he said in something suspiciously close to a growl. Devan released him quickly and turned back to Peyton.

"I hope I didn't interrupt anything."

"No," she said with a flirty laugh. "We were just finishing up. We've got a case to work."

"Well, let me know if you need anything. I aim to be as helpful as possible. I think we're going to have a very good working relationship."

Peyton laughed again and brushed by him, almost bumping into him to get to the door. "Excuse me," she said, bracing her hand on his arm. "See you later, Captain."

Marco flowed out of his chair and exited behind her, not bothering to say goodbye.

Maria stood at her desk, leaning forward to peer into Defino's office as the door closed. "That is one fine piece of man," she breathed.

Peyton glanced back. "Really? I didn't notice."

Marco made a scoffing sound and placed his hands on her shoulders, moving her out of his way. "*I think we're going to have a very good working relationship,*" he mimicked in a fair imitation of Devan's voice. "Wipe the drool off your mouth, Brooks," he called, heading back to his desk.

Peyton took a quick swipe with her fingers, then felt Maria's eyes on her.

"Sure, you didn't notice," said Maria, taking a seat in her desk chair. "Sure, you didn't."

Peyton looked away, then followed Marco back to their desks.

* * *

Peyton got clearance to pull Darla Steven's driver's license records and get her address. She also put a BOLO out on her car once she had the car's license plate number. After grabbing a quick lunch from the coffee shop across the street from the precinct, she and Marco headed out to Darla's Pacific Heights Victorian.

Marco drove. He hadn't said anything to her at lunch, poking at his salad with his fork. As Peyton scarfed down her ham and cheese sandwich, she hadn't worried about his silence. They often went hours without speaking when they were on stakeout, but as they drove to Pacific Heights, she couldn't deny his silence was starting to annoy her.

She could spring her date with Stan on him. She knew that would get a reaction, but she didn't really want him to lecture her about dating at work. Marco had strict rules that he lived by. He didn't believe cops should marry, and he definitely didn't believe they should date anyone they worked with.

"How was your salad?" she asked him. For such a large man, his vegetarianism always amused her, but it was another thing he didn't budge on no matter what.

"Fine."

She tapped her foot on the floor of the Charger. "I could drive, if you want."

"No."

She looked out the passenger window. "Ever think it might be nice working for Google?"

"Nope."

She shifted and speared him with a look. "I'm thinking of getting a neck tattoo that says *hot babe.*"

"Okay."

She smacked him on the arm with the back of her hand. "What's got you all pissy?"

"Nothing."

"I think I can count the number of words you've said to me since we left the precinct. Are you mad at me?"

"Nope."

"Right." She looked back out the window again. "How hot was that ADA?" If nothing else, that should get a rise out of him. Marco wasn't vain, but he wasn't immune to his own looks. He was used to being the most handsome man in a room.

"Guess."

"I mean did you see the way his clothes draped his body? Bet that guy has a six-pack all right. And he's smart and he's probably got money and he smells delicious."

Marco stopped at a light and shifted, staring at her. She could see the annoyed set of his mouth. Finally, she'd gotten a response out of him.

"Why do you have to ride Bob Anderson the way you do?"

"What?" She was shocked by the anger in his voice.

"He almost struck you."

"No, he didn't."

"Peyton!"

Peyton flinched. She hated when he called her
Peyton. It usually meant he was upset with her. "He just
stood up. He's too much of a coward to ever strike me. He
knows I'll shoot him in the balls."

"And Holmes? You're always provoking him."

"Look, D'Angelo, both of those men are threatened
by a woman cop."

"I know, so let's make them feel even more
threatened."

She frowned at him. Where was this coming from?
"You really are mad at me, aren't you?"

He started the Charger moving again. "I'm not mad at
you. It scares me." He gritted out the words. "What if I'm not
there the time one of them snaps?"

"I can take care of myself, Marco."

He chewed on his inner lip. "I'll bet Darla Stevens
thought that too."

CHAPTER 3

Darla, what's up? It's Dave. Just thought I'd give you a call and see if you wanna meet for a drink or something. I'm in town for another few days. I had a great time the other night. Sure wouldn't mind seeing you again before I head back to Dallas. Call me when you get the chance. I'll be up late, thinking about you.

*   *   *

Marco found a parking space two doors down from Darla Stevens' address. They both climbed out of the car and Peyton scanned the license plates on the cars on either side of the street. They were looking for a Nissan Leaf. Besides a multitude of Priuses, Peyton saw at least three Leafs, but none matched Darla's midnight blue color. They also didn't match Darla's license plate number. What the hell!

The Victorian was a three story beauty with gingerbread shingles in a periwinkle blue. The rest of the house was pale blue. This woman had liked her blue. They climbed the stairs and Peyton peered in the window next to the door. It opened onto a square entry hall with a round table in the middle and a split staircase leading to the upper story. On a hunch, she tried the handle, but the door didn't open.

"Think we can break out the window without doing too much damage?" she asked her partner.

"God, I hate to do that. So much paperwork." He looked around the stairs. "Maybe she hid a key."

"I could try one of the neighbors."

"Let's look down in the yard first, okay?"

They descended the steps and searched through the postage-card sized yard, looking for any sign that Darla had left a key in the planter beds. As they looked, a red Toyota

27

Prius pulled into the driveway and a woman dressed in a sharp skirt and blazer got out.

She stood about five seven, model thin, with fashionably curled blond hair and big blue doe eyes. Peyton stopped looking for the key and watched the woman hurry up the walkway, her purse slung over her arm. Peyton noticed the purse and the woman's six inch heels matched her suit perfectly.

"Can I help you?" she said, stopping on the walkway.

Marco rose to his full height and turned, his expression unreadable, but Peyton knew this woman was exactly the kind he liked – tall, curvy, blond – a perfect Barbie doll. She sighed and reached for her badge.

"Inspector Peyton Brooks and this is my partner, Inspector Marco D'Angelo."

To Peyton's surprise, the woman's eyes filled with tears. "Is it true?"

"Is what true?"

"Is Darla dead? I got a call from Lori Hardy and she said…" The woman waved her hand in front of her face as if she were trying to stave off the tears. "She said she found Darla."

Peyton and Marco exchanged a look. Damn it, Peyton had been very clear with Lori that she wasn't to talk with anyone until they'd had a chance to notify next of kin. "Can I ask who you are?"

"I'm Julia Walters, or Jules. Darla and I were best friends."

"Okay, Ms. Walters. Would you happen to know if Darla left a key out here? We have a warrant to search her house, but we'd rather not break the window to get inside."

"I have a key." She started to rummage in her purse. "Oh, wait. I guess I need to see the warrant."

Marco pulled it out of his back pocket and held it out to her with a snap. She took it and opened it, scanning it. Peyton gave Marco a puzzled look. He was obviously still angry at her because he hadn't seemed to notice how pretty

Julia Walters was. Usually, he'd be only too quick to comfort a damsel like her.

She folded it and handed it back, tears and mascara streaking down her face. "She's really dead."

"Look, Ms. Walters…"

"Jules, please."

"Jules, can we go in and talk?" Peyton motioned to the stairs.

"Of course," said Jules, going back to rummaging in her purse. She finally found the keys and went before them up the stairs to unlock the door. As they stepped into the entryway, Peyton could feel the vastness of the structure. According to the internet, it was three stories tall with six bedrooms, eight bathrooms, and a bonus room. Peyton couldn't understand why Darla needed this much space.

She motioned to the kitchen just visible down the hallway off the entrance. "Jules, please go sit in the kitchen and wait for us. We're going to check out the rest of the house. Don't touch anything, please."

Jules nodded, trying to swallow her tears. "Can I at least get a tissue? Darla kept them in the bathroom down here."

"Yes, get a tissue, then touch nothing else."

Jules went off, her head bowed, her shoulders rounded in grief. Peyton turned to Marco. "Call Bob Anderson and have him canvass this house for evidence. I'd call him, but I don't think he's talking to me."

"On it," Marco said, taking out his phone. "Which floor do you want?"

"I'll go up to the second, you do the third. We'll just make sure the place is secure, then meet in the kitchen. I don't want to touch anything until Bob's had a chance to take some pictures." Peyton looked around the stylishly decorated mansion. "I know she sold high end properties, but what the hell did Darla need with such a massive house?"

Marco shook his head. "I'm wondering the same thing. Did you notice if she was wearing a wedding ring?"

"I didn't, but I'll bet Jules will know. Let's do a preliminary sweep and meet back down here."

They found no one in any of the rooms. There didn't appear to be any sign of struggle and nothing was obviously amiss. Only one bedroom looked like it was being used: a towel hung a little crooked on the holder, a book lay on the nightstand by the bed, some garbage sat in the garbage can next to the toilet. The rest of the house looked like a museum, as if no one had ever lived here before.

Peyton and Marco met in the entrance hallway a few moments later. "Bob's on his way," said Marco, "but I don't think he's gonna find anything."

Peyton agreed. They knew she'd been killed in the Painted Lady, but whoever killed her had probably not met her here in this house. The way everything looked, Peyton found it hard to believe anyone besides Darla lived here and even then, it seemed she used it mostly for a crash pad, nothing more.

"I didn't see any signs of a man. No clothes in the closet in the bedroom, no razor, no other male stuff," said Peyton, moving toward the kitchen. "Does this place have a garage?"

"I think so. I'll go look. You think the car might be in there?"

"I think we better check everything."

"You see a purse in her room?"

"Nope."

Marco veered off to the right down a hallway as Peyton entered the great room, a combination family room/kitchen. It had obviously been remodeled because great rooms were a modern invention and this Victorian had to be nearly 100 years old.

Jules sat at the table, her head braced on a hand, staring at her cell phone. Her eyes were rimmed with mascara. Peyton glanced around. The kitchen had all the latest stainless steel appliances, a restaurant grade range and refrigerator. The family room sported sleek blue microfiber couches and a massive flat screen television. Peyton marked there were no photos of people, just landscapes. There hadn't been any photos in the bedroom either.

Going to the refrigerator, she opened it. Besides a jar of pickles and a number of bottles of flavored water, there didn't seem to be any food in here. Pulling open a vegetable drawer, she found a take-out box, but that was it. A wine fridge next to the range was full and a wine rack hung on the wall in the breakfast nook. It too was filled. No beer, no hard alcohol.

She felt Jules' eyes on her as she made her rounds. Pulling open the cabinet under the sink, she looked for Darla's trashcan, but she didn't find it. Beyond a couple of cleaning supplies, the cabinet was bare. Turning a circle, she tried to see if there was an external can.

"She had a trash compactor. It's next to the sink," said Jules. "It looks just like the rest of the cabinets."

"Thank you," said Peyton, pulling it open. It was nearly empty. A few discarded paper towels, some take-out boxes, a couple of empty envelopes. She'd wait for Bob to come before she looked any further.

Marco returned to the kitchen. "No car."

Peyton nodded, then faced Jules. Walking over to the table, she took a seat as Marco prowled around the room. "Do you mind if I take notes while we talk?" she asked the woman.

Jules' attention kept wandering to Marco, but she shook her head. "Fine."

Peyton took out her notebook and removed the pen, clicking it on. "Tell me your name again."

"Julia Walters, but everyone always calls me Jules."

"Okay."

"Is Darla dead?" The huge eyes grew liquid again. "Please tell me Lori was wrong."

Peyton laid her hand on Jules'. "I'm so sorry, Jules. Darla is dead."

A sob choked in her throat and she lifted the tissue to wipe the tears away.

"You said you and Darla were best friends?"

"Right. We went to college together. We took our real estate license exam together. We've even been on vacation together."

"So you're a realtor too?"

Jules nodded. "Darla and I had these silly competitions. We were going for drinks tonight." She stopped suddenly and the tears overflowed.

Peyton waited for her to calm herself, looking over at her partner. Marco had stopped roaming the family room and turned to give her a disgusted look. Marco wasn't the most patient man when it came to weepy females.

Jules eventually calmed. "I'm sorry," she said, wiping her eyes and blowing her nose.

"No problem," said Peyton. "So you were going for drinks tonight because…"

"She got the listing for the Painted Lady and I got a listing on Mason. Seven million. It was going to make my year."

"I'll bet."

"I can't believe this happened."

"How long has she had the listing for the Painted Lady?"

"Only about a week. I think she's had a few showings. She hasn't even held an open house yet."

Peyton gave her a skeptical look. "An open house? For a house worth millions?"

"Well, it isn't like you think. It's very exclusive. Only by invitation."

"I see."

"Darla was always so careful. She always checked out the people she showed houses to. You know how it is? It can be scary in this business. Going into an empty house by yourself at all hours." She glanced over at Marco, then leaned close to Peyton. "I carry pepper spray."

"That's good," said Peyton. "That's good. Always better to be prepared."

Jules nodded.

"Do you know who Darla would have shown the house to?"

"Oh, there's bound to be a list in her office. All of that is carefully logged on the computer."

"Right. Can you give me the address to her office?" She pushed the pad over to Jules. Jules wrote and passed it back.

"We're in the same building."

"Good." Peyton tapped the pen against the pad. "So, was Darla married?"

Jules gave a snort of disgust. "Divorced."

"You sound like you don't care for her husband."

Jules looked over at Marco again, but he'd wandered from the room. "He was an asshole."

"Abusive?"

"Verbally. I hated him. I always told her he was why I'd never marry."

"Can you tell me his name?"

"Gerald. Gerald Stevens. He's a real estate broker. Thinks he's a big freakin' deal."

"So he's in San Francisco?" said Peyton, writing the name.

"Yeah, he has a condo on Russian Hill, bought it after the divorce. Darla kept the house."

Peyton glanced around at the mansion. "So this was their house?"

"Yeah."

"It's huge," said Peyton, giving Jules a bewildered look.

"Ridiculous, isn't it? I told her to sell. I told her to get one of those new condos down in the Marina, but she wouldn't think about it."

Peyton tapped the pen some more. "Was she seeing anyone?"

"Yeah, she was seeing some guy named Dave. I can't remember his last name. He lives in Dallas." Again Jules looked around for Marco before she leaned close to Peyton. "I think he's married. He was out here just a few days ago, but he might have gone back. I don't know." Jules pressed the tissue under her eye. "I wasn't too impressed with him either. Darla sure knew how to pick 'em."

Peyton wrote down Dave's name, then Dallas and put a question mark after it. Looking up at Jules, she found the woman tearing up again as the realization of her friend's death ambushed her. "Jules, I know this is hard."

"Harder than you can imagine," she said, blowing her nose.

"Is there anyone who might have wanted to do Darla harm? A jealous agent? Any other men in her life?"

"I can't think of anyone." She pointed a finger at Peyton, her eyes red rimmed. "I'll bet you money it was that husband of hers. He's a mean bastard. He couldn't believe she would leave him."

"We'll look into it, don't worry about that, but…" Peyton reached into her pocket and took out her business card, passing it to the woman. "If you think of anything else, will you let me know?"

Jules took it, nodding. "I'll let you know."

"Thank you," Peyton said, rising to her feet to let Jules know the conversation was over.

Jules rose also, hitching her purse onto her shoulder. "Goodbye," she said, then hurried from the room, sidestepping as Marco came back in.

Peyton gave him an arch look. "Thanks a lot for helping me question her."

"Hey, I went out to meet Bob. Let's just say I had to promise to keep you two rooms away from him at all times."

Peyton made a scoffing noise. "He's afraid of a girl, D'Angelo, really?"

Marco dropped his arm around her shoulders and steered her toward the front door. "We all are, Brooks, we all are," he said.

* * *

The next morning, Peyton's cell phone rang as she was pouring herself a cup of coffee. It startled her in the quiet of her little kitchen. She'd gotten used to the silence. She hated it, but she'd gotten used to it. As she reached for the phone, she wondered if she shouldn't get a dog. A dog would make the little house less lonely, less empty, especially now that her father was gone. A dog made a home, right?

She glanced at the display and saw Abe's name flash at her. She thumbed it on, taking a sip of her coffee. "Good morning, Abe."

"Good morning, little soul sista, how are you, sweets?"

"Fine. What do you think about me getting a dog?"

Abe fell silent. "As in a yapping, pooping member of the canine family?"

"Yep."

"I think they're overrated."

"Really? You wouldn't like a poodle that you could groom into puffballs with bows in its hair."

"Hm, now that you mention it, I could have a righteous dog. Can you imagine the accessories I could get for him? And I could paint his toenails hot pink."

"See, now you're in the spirit."

"I could see you with a dog, toots. Some feisty little terrier with more personality than size, yep, that would suit you just fine."

Peyton laughed. Yes, she was going to get a dog. She'd been talking about it for months, but now that she was about to buy the house, it just seemed like a responsible, adult thing to do.

A horn honked from the driveway.

"Hey, Abe, Marco's here. You call for any specific reason?" She fixed the lid on her travel cup and grabbed the one she'd prepared for him, then she hurried to the door, setting both on the sofa table. Grabbing up her badge, she affixed it to her belt, then slid her thin wallet with her license and bank cards into her pocket. Finally, she snatched up her keys and the two coffees, opening the door and stepping outside.

"I completed the autopsy on your realtor this morning."

Peyton balanced both cups in one hand and shut the door, locking it. She had the phone wedged between her shoulder and ear, the strap of her gun holster rubbing against her neck. "And?"

"Strangulation. You wanna come by and I can show you?"

"Nope, I'm good." She jogged down the stairs. As she appeared around the corner of her house, Marco rolled down the Charger's window and took the coffee cup from her.

"Morning," he said, taking a sip.

"Morning," she called back, hurrying around the front of the car.

"Is that my D-licious Angel I hear?" said Abe.

"You know it is." She opened the door and slipped into the seat, setting the coffee cup in the holder and slipping her keys into her pocket, then she reached for the seatbelt. "Back to Darla Stevens."

"Right."

"We guessed she'd been strangled. Do you have anything else for us?"

Marco put the Charger in reverse and backed to the end of the driveway. It was always a little tricky getting out onto 19th, especially in the morning, but Marco did it like a pro.

"She had broken fingernails, and scratch marks on her neck above the ligature marks."

"She fought?"

"She tried to stop whoever it was from strangling her."

"Please tell me there was DNA under her fingernails?"

"Nope. Just fibers from whatever item strangled her. I'm assuming it was a silk scarf based on the fibers, but I sent the fibers to the lab to be evaluated. Did you find a scarf or anything at the scene?"

Peyton watched Marco deftly turn toward the precinct. "No, I'm afraid he might have taken the scarf for a souvenir."

Abe was silent for a moment. Finally, he cleared his throat. "That's disturbing, sweets."

"I know."

"You're not thinking a serial killer."

"Not with one murder, but I don't like the missing murder weapon or her car and purse." She sipped at her coffee, bracing her hand on the dashboard as Marco made another turn. "Anything else? What about a tox screen? Was she drugged?"

"No."

"Sexually assaulted?"

"No, again." She could hear Abe fussing with papers on his end. "Here's the thing, Peyton. It takes at least two minutes to strangle someone to death. Now that might not seem like a long time, but think about it."

Peyton shivered. "I try not to think about those things, Abe."

"He had to have gotten her from behind, pulled the scarf tight, and held on until she stopped fighting, losing consciousness."

A thought jumped to the front of Peyton's mind. "Can you estimate the size of the man we're looking for?"

"Not with what I have. He wouldn't have had to be taller than her if he got the drop on her. He wouldn't have had to be that much bigger than her at all. With the scarf already around her neck and if he was behind her, he just needed leverage."

"Okay. Send your report to my email."

"Already done, sweets. You sure you don't want to come down and view my work personally?"

"I'll pass."

"More's the pity. I'm really quite talented, you know?"

"I know, you tell me all the time."

The radio crackled, the dispatcher asking for their location. Marco picked up the mic and answered her.

"Abe, I gotta go," she said as the dispatcher came back, informing them that a midnight blue Nissan Leaf had been found abandoned at Fort Funston.

"Talk to you later, sugarbeets," Abe said and disconnected the call as Marco made the next turn to take them out toward the ocean.

"Have them repeat the license plate number on the car," Peyton told Marco.

He relayed her message to the dispatcher. The radio crackled, then the woman came on the line, reading out the series of digits and letters. Peyton checked it against her notebook as the dispatcher spoke.

"That's it," she said, nodding.

"So, Abe determined she was strangled to death?"

"That's what he said. Her fingernails were broken, but he only got traces of silk fiber with a scrape."

"No sexual assault?"

"No."

"Could it be a woman?"

Peyton shifted in her seat, giving him a narrow-eyed look. "You mean a rival?"

"Yeah. What if one of her sister realtors wasn't happy she got the listing for the Painted Lady?"

"That's an interesting idea, D'Angelo," she said, pondering it. She made some notes in her notepad. "Maybe we better take a closer look at your Barbie doll."

"What?" He gave her a bewildered look. "What Barbie doll?"

"Jules Walters?"

"The woman from yesterday?"

"That's the one."

"Why is she *my* Barbie doll?"

Peyton made a choked sound. "Seriously? She's exactly the sort of woman you'd take to bed."

He gave her a disgusted shake of his head. "I don't have *a sort of woman*."

"You have a type."

"And you? What's your type? Tall, dark, and financially loaded?"

Peyton shrugged, looking out the front window. "I'm not gonna lie. That type is tempting."

Marco pretended to shove his finger down his throat, gagging.

She hit him in the shoulder, but she was smiling. "You're impossible."

He reached over and ruffled her hair. She batted his hand away, then smoothed out her ponytail.

They arrived at Fort Funston twenty minutes later. Peyton spotted the blue Nissan Leaf immediately, parked in a parking space, a uniform standing by it. Marco pulled up behind it and they got out. The uniform walked over to them, holding out her hand.

"You must be Brooks and D'Angelo," she said, shaking hands with Peyton, then Marco. She was middle aged, Latino, dark hair tucked under her hat. "I'm Sanchez."

"Officer Sanchez, thanks for calling it in," said Peyton as Marco wandered over to the car, peering inside. He already had his phone in his hand, texting someone. Peyton figured it was probably Bob Anderson, so he could go over the car for evidence. "How did you find it?"

"I was patrolling out here this morning and I spotted it. I remembered the BOLO. It's the car you were looking for, right?"

"Right. You got a slim jim in your vehicle?"

Sanchez walked over to her patrol car and grabbed something out of the passenger side as Peyton went back to the Charger and took two pairs of latex gloves from the glove compartment. She handed a pair to Marco and began pulling on her own, while she watched Sanchez jimmy the lock.

When the click sounded, Marco opened the driver's door as Peyton went around to the passenger side. Searching the interior, Peyton didn't immediately see anything out of place, but she didn't want to crawl inside until Bob Anderson had a chance to go over it.

"No purse?" said Marco, glancing up at her.

"Pop the trunk," said Peyton, nodding to the button on the driver's side.

Marco popped the trunk. Together they walked to the back and Marco pushed it open. An expensive designer handbag sat on the dark carpeting. Marco gave her a lift of his brows.

"Good guess, Brooks."

Peyton eyed the bag, shaking her head. "She had an appointment to meet someone at that house, Marco."

"Why do you say that?"

"A woman puts her purse in the trunk when she knows she won't need it, but she doesn't want to carry it around." She turned, pointing her gloved finger at him. "I'll just bet whoever killed her is on her appointment calendar."

Marco removed his phone again. "I'll get started on a warrant for her office then."

* * *

Peyton and Stan walked into the pizza parlor and found a seat near the window. Stan held out her chair and Peyton slid into it, hiding her smile. He'd shown up at her house with a box of chocolates and a bouquet of flowers. She loved the chocolates, but she could have done without the flowers. It was just something for her to watch wilt. Still, it was sweet and she'd kissed him on the cheek for it. He'd blushed so furiously, Peyton worried he might have a stroke.

Now he sat down across from her, giving her a goofy grin. He wore a collared shirt, not his usual t-shirt, buttoned all the way to the top, a pair of tight jeans, and his usual Converse sneakers. He'd tried to tame his brown hair, parting it on the side and slicking it back with…well, she didn't know what and she wasn't going to ask. The candle in the middle of the table flickered under his glasses, making his eyes look like two black holes in his face.

Peyton had tried to be conservative. She wore her usual leather jacket, a blue t-shirt and jeans, but she'd taken her hair down. It formed a curtain of curls to the middle of her back. She'd caught Stan brushing the backs of his fingers over it when he'd helped her put on her jacket at the house.

"Thank you for inviting me, Stan," she said.

"Thank you for coming, Peyton." He beamed at her again. "You look awesome."

She wasn't dressed any differently than any other day, but she smiled back at him. "Thank you."

The pizza parlor was moderately crowded, a lot of men sitting at the bar, watching a basketball game on the television over the order window. Every once in a while a cheer would go up from the group. A couple of families and a few couples sat at tables in the dining area, eating pizzas, and a group of teenagers were playing video games in the back corner.

A waitress appeared, a teenage girl, smacking on a wad of gum. "What'll it be?"

"Order whatever you want, Peyton."

Peyton fought a laugh. Stan was pulling out all the stops – pizza, beer, chocolates, flowers – what more could a girl want? "What about a combination?" she suggested.

"Sounds awesome." He looked up at the bored girl. "We'll have a large combo and a pitcher of beer." He gave

Peyton a hopeful nod. Peyton nodded back. "Yeah, a pitcher of beer."

"Sure." With a flounce of her blond hair, she turned and walked away.

Stan sat on his hands, staring at her so intently, Peyton wanted to squirm.

"So do you come to this place a lot, Stan?"

"Naw, my roommate suggested it. He said the pizza's good."

"Your roommate?"

"Doug, Doug Brown. We went to college together."

"Really? Where did you go to school, Stan?"

"Cal Poly Pomona. I studied computer forensics."

"So when you came to San Francisco, Doug came too?"

"Yeah, he works from home, but he's employed by a computer gaming company in the Silicon Valley." He laughed. "We get to try out all the new games before they go on the market."

"Cool."

"Yeah."

The waitress returned and set the pitcher and two plastic cups on the table, then she walked away without saying anything. Stan poured the beer into the glasses, spilling some on the table as well. Peyton grabbed a napkin out of the holder and wiped it up. She noticed his hands were shaking as he pushed a glass toward her.

Peyton took a sip of her beer, hoping he'd do the same and calm down. He lifted his own glass and sipped, his face twisting into a grimace. Peyton hid her smile, setting her glass down. Stan clearly wasn't a beer drinker.

"Do you play video games?" he said.

Peyton shook her head. "Not often, no."

He sat back, clearly disappointed. He probably thought he'd hit on something they could share. "You have a computer?"

"Yeah, a laptop, but it's mostly for email."

"Do you go on social media?"

"You mean Facebook?"

"Facebook, Twitter, Pinterest?"

Peyton sighed. "No, not really. I don't have much time and I don't know, it's not really my thing."

"Yeah, I guess not. I mean, your life is pretty exciting as it is. You don't need that stuff."

"It's not that," she said, reaching for the salt shaker and twirling it. "I just work a lot and when I'm home, I just wanna do something else."

"Yeah." He looked down at the table. "You probably go on a lot of dates, right?"

Peyton ran her fingers down the salt shaker. "Dates?" Ha! She hadn't been on a date in more than a year. "No, not really."

He looked up at her, the candle light flickering in his glasses. "Really? I can't believe that."

"Why?"

"Because you're you and well, look at you." He threw out his hand, obviously trying to motion at her appearance, but he hit his glass of beer and sent it sprawling across the table. "Oh no!"

Peyton picked up the empty glass. "Don't worry about it. I'll just get a rag from the bar." She pushed back her chair and hurried to the bar. She hated to see the panicked, crestfallen look on Stan's face. He was trying so hard to make this a good date for her, but he was just so damn nervous.

She moved to an open spot at the bar next to a guy in a cowboy hat. *Boy, there were all kinds in San Francisco,* she thought. He turned and gave her a slow perusal, but she ignored him, motioning to the bartender.

"Hey, sugar," said the cowboy, jerking his chin at her.

"Hey," she said, shooting him a back-the-hell-off look.

He leaned back on his barstool and took a long look at her backside. "Why don't you park that cute little ass right here?" He patted his thighs, swiping his tongue over his lips and winking at her.

Peyton ignored him as the bartender started to move in her direction.

"A sweet little ass like that would fit just perfect." He made a motion with his hands as if he were squeezing her butt cheeks. Peyton glared at him, but before she could tell him to go screw himself, Stan stepped up and tapped him on the shoulder.

"Don't talk to my date that way!" he said, clenching his fist at his side.

"What?" asked the cowboy, giving Stan a disparaging look. "Seriously?"

Peyton stepped between Stan and the cowboy, placing her hands on Stan's shoulders to back him up. "It's okay. Go back to our table and I'll be right there."

"He shouldn't talk to you like that!" Stan thrust out his chin.

The cowboy swiveled his barstool around and rose to his feet, towering over the two of them. Peyton could feel the tension ratchet up in the room as the rest of the bar went silent.

"Stan, it's okay."

"No! Tell her you're sorry," Stan ordered. "Tell her or I swear…"

Peyton could feel the cowboy looming behind her, but she focused on Stan.

"Or what?" said the cowboy.

Stan's mouth worked, but nothing came out.

"Or I'll toss your ass through that window and into the street!" said the cowboy, pointing to the plate glass window on their left.

Stan pushed against Peyton's hands. "You just try!"

Peyton closed her eyes briefly, but when the cowboy reached around her for Stan, she knew she had to react. Grabbing her badge out of her coat pocket, she whirled and shoved it in the cowboy's face.

"Enough!" she barked, drawing all eyes in the room to her. "Sit your ass down and drink your beer before I arrest you for assaulting an officer!"

The cowboy took a step back and one of his buddies put his hand on his shoulder, backing him up another step. "Leave it alone!" said the friend.

The cowboy held up his hands. "No problem, Officer," he said, glancing at her badge. "No problem."

Peyton released her held breath and replaced her badge as the cowboy took his seat again, turning his back on the two of them. Peyton shifted and grabbed Stan's arm, leading him back to the table. Stan meekly followed her, taking his seat again, then he grabbed her glass and downed half of it in one swallow, shivering at the taste. Peyton sat down across from him, watching him as his face turned red. She suspected this was more beer than Stan had ever drank in his life and she was probably going to have to drive them home. She hated that she'd humiliated him when he was trying to be her hero, but she couldn't let the cowboy take a swing at him. He might knock poor Stan's head clean off.

To her surprise, Stan leaned close to her and his eyes glittered in the candlelight. "That was so cool!" he said. "Total badassery!"

Badassery? Peyton gave him a bewildered look. "What?"

"You! You're a badass, Peyton. But you know what would have been better?"

Yeah, not having a confrontation in a pizza parlor. "No, what?" she asked skeptically.

"If you'd pulled your gun," he said, then gave a weird little breathless pant and fired off two finger guns.

Peyton swallowed hard and leaned away from him, trying not to be obvious about it. *All righty then*, she thought.

This night was so over.

CHAPTER 4

Darla, it's Deb. I just heard something on the news that has me spooked. Please call me back. I'm really worried. They said they found a woman murdered in a house while she was showing a client. Darla, please pick up! You know how much I worry about you and that job! Call me as soon as you get this message!

* * *

Marco picked Peyton up the next morning. As was their usual routine, she carried him a cup of coffee in his travel mug and passed it to him through the window. He took it, immediately taking a sip. She knew she didn't have to bring him coffee, he was perfectly capable of brewing it himself, but since she made a cup for herself, it only seemed reasonable that she bring one for him.

She sank into the passenger seat. "Morning," she said, smiling at him.

"Morning," he said, setting the cup in the holder and putting the car in reverse. "How was your night?"

"Good," she said, deliberately avoiding any mention of the disastrous date with Stan. She knew he'd tease her about it, then the whole precinct would know and Stan would be embarrassed. Stan was a sweet guy and she didn't want him being the butt of anyone's joke. Besides that, she didn't need any crap from Marco. Long ago, they'd promised not to interfere in each other's sex life and she didn't want to break that rule now.

"So, what's on the agenda for today?" he asked.

Peyton curled her hands around the coffee mug and breathed in the steam. God, she loved the smell of coffee in the morning, especially on mornings like this where the fog had rolled into the City and didn't look like it would burn off any time soon. "Did Bob Anderson find any evidence in Darla Stevens' car?"

"He found a partial fingerprint. He thinks the perp tried to wipe off the steering wheel, but he missed a spot on the underside."

"Is it enough to run through the system?"

"He's gonna try, but I don't think he'll get anything."

"Then I first want to talk to the ex-husband. He lives on Russian Hill. I called him first thing this morning and told him we'd be over about 9:00."

"You got an address?"

Peyton pulled her notebook out of her jacket pocket and showed it to him. He took it, bracing it on the dashboard.

"Call Maria and let her know where we're headed," he told Peyton.

She made a face. She hated checking in with Maria. Maria could never just take a message. She always had to make a snide comment. Fishing out her phone, Peyton dialed the precinct. Maria didn't answer. Peyton breathed a sigh of relief and left a message, then she hung up before Maria could intercept the call.

Marco chuckled. "You got lucky."

"Once in a while I do," she said, staring out at the fog. Maybe they'd get some sun on Russian Hill. "I've got Holmes trying to track down the boyfriend. Dave No-last-name. And hopefully, we'll have our warrant to search her office in a few hours. If Holmes can't get the boyfriend's last name from her co-workers, or we can't get it from her ex-husband, maybe we can get it off her phone."

"What about questioning Jules again?"

"Your Barbie doll?"

He gave her an annoyed look.

Peyton laughed. "Sure, we should talk to her again."

"Did Bob Anderson get the warrant for Darla's phone?"

Peyton shrugged. "I don't know. You get to make that call. He probably has my number blocked."

Marco shook his head in amusement. "Poor guy. He's just trying to make a living, Brooks. You don't have to ride him all the time."

"He sucks, D'Angelo. If he got better at his job, I wouldn't have to ride him."

"Just saying, you get more flies with honey."

"And you get ants too. I don't need ants in my honey."

* * *

A doorman buzzed Gerald Stevens' condo from the lobby. Peyton and Marco stood on the opposite side of the reception counter, looking around the building. Peyton had never seen so much polished chrome. She'd never seen a doorman before either.

"Mr. Stevens says to go right up. He's on the tenth floor."

Peyton nodded and reaffixed her badge to her belt, then she and Marco went to the elevators. Another young man stood by them, reaching out to push the call button. Marco and Peyton exchanged a look. Both men wore navy blue uniforms, polished black shoes, and a navy cap with a short bill.

The elevator arrived and the attendant held the door until they got inside. "Which floor?" he asked Peyton.

"Ten," she said, somewhat confused.

He leaned into the elevator and pressed the right floor, then stepped back, clasping his hands before him. He gave them a patient smile as the doors closed.

Peyton looked around the interior – marble floor, ornate etched glass mirror, sound-proof tiles in the ceiling, and zebrawood paneling.

"Have you ever seen a place like this before?" she asked Marco.

"Land your lawyer and you might," he said, staring up at the numbers above the door.

Peyton stuck her tongue out at him, but he didn't respond. "Do you suppose that guy spends all day just pushing the button for an elevator?"

"Seems like it."

"How much do you think he makes doing that?"

"More than you, Brooks. More than you," he said, rocking on his heels.

A moment later, the doors opened on a plush hallway with zebrawood accents, thick carpeting, and expensive antique tables with fresh cut flowers sitting on top of them in crystal vases, or maybe it was diamond. As if Peyton would know the difference.

They found Gerald Stevens' condo and knocked on the door. A Latino woman in her late twenties opened it. She wore a maid's uniform, her bountiful assets straining the bodice. The hem of the dress was so short Peyton worried she'd get a peep show.

"Yes?"

Peyton took out her badge and flashed it at the woman. "Inspectors Brooks and D'Angelo to see Mr. Stevens."

"This way," she said, stepping back and motioning them into the palatial condo.

If Peyton thought Darla Stevens' house was impressive, this was more so. The entrance hall opened on a loft style space with exposed steel beams running across the ceiling. A turquoise blue leather couch and two ivory leather armchairs were arranged around a chrome box coffee table with mirrored end tables on either side. Sleek chrome lamps with square lampshades in turquoise sat on the tables, but there were no other items to mar the shiny surface. To the left was a galley kitchen with marble countertops, zebrawood cabinets, and more stainless steel appliances than Peyton would know what to do with. A stainless steel table took up the space before a wall of floor to ceiling windows. Leather chairs were arranged around the table and in the center was a crystal vase bursting with flowers.

A tall man in a business suit paced before the windows, talking loudly on a cell phone. The maid stopped before him, clasping her hands at her back and waiting patiently for him to acknowledge her. The position nearly made her breasts tumble out of her outfit. Finally he turned, spotted his visitors, and waved her off. She gave a slight nod and shifted to face them.

"He'll be right with you," she said, then meandered away past the kitchen and into a hallway, disappearing into a room.

Peyton watched her until she was gone, then took another look around. She just noticed the cowhide rug lying beneath the chrome coffee table. One corner had been accidentally flipped up to show the animal's hide. She shivered and glanced up at Marco.

"Lot of leather."

He kept his gaze fixed on the windows, staring out at the magnificent view of the City. "Yeah, my skin's crawling."

As a devout vegetarian, this place must feel like hell to him. Peyton was a little surprised this guy didn't have a cow's head mounted over his faux fireplace on the wall opposite the couch. While they waited, she decided to focus on the man instead of his decor.

Gerald Stevens had to be in his late thirties, early forties. He had a full head of brown hair, slicked back from a broad forehead with mousse. He wore a business suit in tan, but the jacket lay over one of the chairs around the table. His white shirt sleeves were rolled up to mid-forearm and a Rolex watch shined on his wrist, or Peyton assumed it was a Rolex. She didn't think a man like this would wear a fake. He had a handsome face, but his lips were thin and oddly small, and his eyes seemed a little too wide-spaced.

He yelled into the phone, his words clipped and commanding. This was not a man who expected people to rebel. She couldn't help but wonder if he'd been the same way with his wife. Finally, he barked a goodbye and thumbed the call off, then turned to them, his free hand on his hip.

Motioning with the hand that held the phone, he moved toward them. "Officers, good morning." The smile he shot them would have given a used-car salesman a run for his money. "You would not believe what that call was about."

"It's Inspectors, Mr. Stevens," Peyton corrected mildly.

He stopped, a frown marring his brow. "Right. Inspectors." He held up the phone again. "That was the lawyer for the owners of the Painted Lady. He's very upset that there was a murder in the house. He wants to get a housekeeping service in there, *and* a spiritualist to cleanse it of bad juju."

Peyton blinked in surprise. "Excuse me?"

"He's worried the murder will bring the price down. I told him, Arnold, this is a Painted Lady. An entire Boy Scout troop could be massacred in there and it would still fetch top bank."

Peyton felt her back stiffen and Marco closed his eyes, bowing his head. "Mr. Stevens," she said, "if you'll remember, your ex-wife was the woman murdered in that house. As of this morning, your Painted Lady is a crime scene, so no, we will not be allowing a housekeeper or a spiritualist or a demon slayer to cleanse it of bad juju."

"Demon slayer?"

Peyton's teeth ground together. "I'd like to know where you were yesterday afternoon between the hours of 1:00 and 3:00."

He reared back. "You can't think I did this?" He looked to Marco as if he expected him to take his side. "Really? Me?"

Marco didn't give anything away, just continued to stare at him.

"I find your lack of remorse about your ex-wife's death a bit off, if you want to know the truth," said Peyton.

"Well, I can assure you, Inspector, I am devastated. I mean, Darla and I had our differences, but I never wanted anything like this to happen, especially not in that listing."

Peyton wanted to launch herself at the man and scratch out his eyes, but Marco stepped toward him, laying a hand on his shoulder. "Okay, let's take a seat," he said, directing the man away from her. "We have a few questions we want to ask you." He gave Peyton a stern look and jerked his head toward their suspect.

Peyton reluctantly followed, choosing an armchair across the room from the man for his own safety. Gerald took a seat in the middle of the couch and Marco began his usual wandering, crossing over to the windows and looking out. Peyton was the only one who knew why he did this. It unsettled the person they were questioning and it allowed Marco to absorb everything around him. He often picked up more information from his wandering than Peyton did from her questions.

Gerald sat forward, looking at the display on his phone, his arms braced on his thighs. Peyton reached for her notebook to keep from snatching the damn phone from his hand and throwing it across the room. She already knew she didn't like Gerald Stevens.

"Where were you yesterday afternoon between 1:00 and 3:00?" she repeated.

"I was in my office."

"Can anyone vouch for your whereabouts?"

"My secretary and two of my realtors. I was meeting with them about a new condo complex opening in Emeryville. We were planning a marketing campaign to attract millennials."

"You were there for the entire time?"

"We were there until about 4:20 or so. That's when I got the call that Darla was found in the Painted Lady."

"Does Darla still work for you?"

"She does." He shook his head. "She did. We were divorced. I mean, we didn't work as a couple, but I didn't wish anything bad to happen to her. She was one of my top realtors, and this Painted Lady was really going to set us up for the year."

"Can you give me the names of the realtors you were with yesterday?" She held out her notebook. "I'll need to check your alibi."

"Be happy to." He took the pad and pen, setting the phone on the table. Then he scribbled something, his head bowed over the paper. Peyton couldn't deny it made her happy to see the bald spot on the crown of his head.

Marco had found his way into the kitchen, meandering around, his eyes sweeping over every surface. Gerald didn't even bother to glance his way as he passed back the pad and pen.

"You're not going to find anything, Inspector," Gerald called to Marco. "I'm telling you I had nothing to do with Darla's death."

"Just looking at the fixtures. Might want to do some remodeling," he said.

Peyton had seen Marco's apartment. It definitely needed remodeling. It epitomized the term bachelor pad.

"Do you have any leads?" Gerald asked Peyton.

"Besides you," she said, giving him a lazy smile.

He pretended to laugh. "Darla made me a lot of money, Inspector. Forget we were married. Forget we were divorced. I'm not a man about to bite the hand that feeds me." He motioned around the condo. "As you can see, I like the finer things in life."

"The mansion she has seems like one of the finer things. Maybe you wanted that for yourself."

"That mausoleum? Are you kidding me? I hated that house. I always felt like I was rattling around it in. And something was always going wrong. We dumped so much good money into that ancient piece of shit."

A text flashed on his screen and he reached for the phone, but Peyton leaned forward, holding her hand over it.

"That can wait until we're done."

He seemed to visibly struggle with himself not to snatch it up. Marco had wandered back to the windows, but he glanced over his shoulder, watching Gerald.

"Do you get the house now?"

Gerald shook his head almost wistfully. "It goes to her sister. Everything she had goes to Deb and her three kids."

"Bet that bothered you."

Gerald shrugged. "I'm doing just fine, Inspector. I don't need Darla's money. I needed Darla's ability to sell a house, but I didn't need anything else from her."

"Where does her sister live?"

"South San Francisco. Her kids are eight and five and three, I think. She works in a pharmacy as a pharmacy assistant."

"What's her full name?"

"Debra Lawrence."

"She have any reason to want to get her inheritance early?"

Gerald blew out air, his gaze shifting down to the phone as another text came through, but he didn't reach for it. "Deb and me, we didn't get along so well, but she wouldn't have done this. She and Darla were tight, you know? Man, she lost it when I had to call and tell her what happened."

"So, she's been informed?"

"Yeah, I called her yesterday right after I got the call." He shook his head, turning his wrist to look at his watch. "Man, that was a shock."

"Julia Walters said Darla had a boyfriend."

"Yeah, Dave, um, Dave Forrester. He lives in Dallas."

"How did they meet?"

"In a hotel in St. Louis. They were there for a convention. I think they met in the bar."

"Is he a realtor?"

"No, he's in banking or something. I think he does mortgage loans."

"When did he leave to go back to Dallas?"

Gerald pursed his lips. It wasn't an attractive look on him. "I think he left yesterday morning. You should be able to check his flight."

"We will. We'd also like to see her office. Did she have an appointment book or a client list?"

"Yeah, but all of that would have been on her phone."

"Her friend Jules thought it might be logged into the computer at the office."

"Not her personal appointments. They only get logged after we write a contract. Her initial contacts would be in her phone. Have you gotten a warrant for her phone?"

"Not yet, but we're working on it," said Peyton. "Was there anyone who might have wanted to do Darla harm?"

Gerald straightened, his brow furrowing. "What? Why would anyone want to hurt Darla?"

"Were there any rivalries in the office? Were there any other realtors jealous that she got the listing for the Painted Lady?"

"Jealous? Sure. It's a huge listing, Inspector Brooks. It'll make the year, but no one would want to strangle her for it." He thought for a moment. "No one could be that diabolical."

Peyton didn't respond, making a note on her pad.

"Right? No one would kill someone like that for something so petty."

Peyton glanced up at him. "It's been done before, Mr. Stevens. It's been done many times before."

* * *

After talking with Gerald Stevens, they headed back to the precinct. Marco drove for a while in silence and Peyton let him alone. She was trying to get her head around this case. With so little evidence, there were too many leads. She hated cases where their leads were slim, but she didn't like ones

where there were just too many people who could have
wanted Darla dead.

Maria gave Peyton the evil eye as they entered the
building. Peyton pasted a fake smile on her face, hoping that
it might make Maria reluctant to goad her.

Not a chance in hell.

"My God, Brooks, have you seen that hair? Did you
even bother to run a comb through it?"

Peyton automatically put a hand on her ponytail,
hating herself for it. She forced herself not to run to the
bathroom to check. It had been windy on Russian Hill. Still
she hadn't thought to fix her hair when they got back to the
Charger.

Maria's attention had already shifted to her partner.
"Captain Defino would like an update, baby, when you get
the chance."

They both looked toward Defino's closed office door.
"You wanna update her now?" Marco asked Peyton.

Peyton shook her head. "I wanna grab the whiteboard
and write all the suspects down, then see where we are. We
need to get the warrant for her phone and one for her office.
If we get the one for her office, we can verify Gerald's alibi."

Marco nodded. "I'll go grab us a couple cups of
coffee. You tell the captain we're gonna map it all out in the
conference room."

"Got it. Stop by Bob Anderson's cubicle and see if he
can check on the warrants."

"Sure thing."

They parted and Peyton made her way toward
Defino's door. She gave Maria a puzzled look. "That's an
interesting color on you," she said, nodding at Maria's blouse.
It had a flouncy scarf that looked like it might be made of
silk, but it was also canary yellow and turned Maria's brown
skin a little sallow. "You look like an ear of corn."

Maria glanced down at herself, making Peyton beam
just a little. It felt good to get back at the hateful receptionist.

Peyton knocked on the door, keeping an eye on Maria so she didn't launch over the desk at her.

"Enter," came Defino's voice.

Peyton poked her head inside the office. "Hey, Captain, Marco and I are going to plot the case on the whiteboard in the conference room. You wanna watch?"

She realized, too late, that Defino wasn't alone. The handsome ADA Devan Adams sat in the farthest chair from Defino's desk.

"Hello, Inspector Brooks," he said in his smooth as velvet voice. He rose to his feet and held out his hand. "How are you?"

When she gave him her hand, he clasped his other one over the top. Peyton felt a flutter of pleasure rush through her. Damn, it had been too long since she dated anyone. "I'm fine," she said. "How are you?"

"Very well, thank you." He finally released her. "By the way, I think your hair looks fantastic."

Peyton again touched her ponytail. "Oh," she said a little breathlessly, "thank you."

"We'll be right in, Brooks," said Defino, but Peyton didn't pay attention to her.

She found herself mesmerized by this man. His cologne was subtle, but she liked the scent, and he was dressed impeccably, his shoes shining. He flashed a brilliant white smile at her, his eyes crinkling at the corners.

"Brooks?" said Defino.

Peyton blinked. "Right. Right," she said, taking a step back. "See you soon."

"See you soon, Inspector Brooks," said Devan.

Peyton pulled the door closed at her back and leaned against it. She found both Marco and Maria staring at her.

"What?" she said.

"You got it bad, Brooks," said Marco, shaking his head.

"Yeah, she does, but what the hell is wrong with him?" added Maria. "Your hair looks like a rat's nest."

Peyton gave her a placid look. Nothing Maria said was going to find its mark now. "Jealousy is so unbecoming, Maria. Don't worry. You're still my number one girl." Then she walked toward Marco, taking the coffee cup from his hand. "And you? Did you put enough sugar in it?"

He gave a chuckle. "You know I did. I emptied the whole damn dispenser into it, Brooks," he said, following her into the conference room.

* * *

Peyton picked up the dry erase marker and studied the blank board. Marco took a seat at the head of the table, closest to her. "What did Bob say about the warrants?"

"He's checking. Stan requested the one for the phone, but he hasn't gotten it yet."

Peyton nodded, distracted. She stepped forward and wrote *Gerald Stevens* on the board, then *ex-husband* and *alibi* with a question mark after it. "Always start with the ex."

"Right."

She tapped the base of the marker against her lower lip. "But I don't think he did it. He's an ass, but I just don't think he did it."

"Why not?"

"I think he was telling us the truth when he said he liked the money she brought in. He's a real estate broker. He wants the commission."

"I agree."

Peyton wrote *Julia Walters* below Gerald's name, then *best friend*. After that she wrote *potential rival*. "I should have gotten an alibi from her, but she seemed so broken up about Darla's death."

"That's why we follow up, Brooks." Marco swiveled the chair back and forth with a booted foot. He lounged in the chair, his long-sleeved t-shirt straining across his chest.

Next Peyton wrote *Dave Forrester, boyfriend, Dallas* and finally, *Debra Lawrence, sister, inheritance*. Stepping back, she studied her board. "I wonder if there are any other rivals in the office?"

"Gerald didn't say how many people worked for him?"

Peyton shook her head. "I figured we'd find that out when we got the warrant."

"Right. Add the partial fingerprint from the car, the car being parked at Fort Funston, and her purse in the trunk."

Peyton made the notations as he asked, setting the cap on the pen but not securing it tightly. "We really need that warrant for her phone records. If we add in her clients, this list could get really out of hand."

"Maybe not," said Marco, still swiveling in his chair. "With the high end houses she sold, maybe there won't be many clients."

"Hm." Peyton tapped the marker against her lip once more, considering what he said.

"Well, that's a lot of suspects and very little evidence," came a masculine voice.

Peyton whipped her head around, knocking off the cap on the top of the marker. Devan and Defino stood just inside the doorway. "We're just waiting on warrants for Darla's phone and office. If we check out Gerald's alibi, look into the time of the boyfriend's flight, and get an alibi from Julia, we can cross three off the list."

Defino squinted at her, but that wasn't unusual. "Where are we on the warrants?"

Peyton shrugged. "We don't have them yet."

Looking up at Devan, Defino gave him a pointed stare. He reached into his pocket and pulled out his phone. "I'll see if I can speed it along," he said, pressing a button and holding the phone to his ear. He turned and moved toward the doorway, but he glanced over at Peyton, motioning to his cheek.

Peyton narrowed her eyes in confusion, but Defino just turned and followed him out. Looking over at Marco, she shrugged. "What?"

Marco gave a laugh and rose to his feet, tilting her chin up. "You've got something on the corner of your mouth."

Peyton's hand flew to her face. "What?"

"Drool," he said, chucking her under the chin.

"Drool?"

He laughed. "God, you're so easy, Brooks. No, you tagged yourself with the marker when you launched the cap at me." Patting her on the head, he walked around her toward the door, still chuckling.

Peyton felt a flush of humiliation rush through her and she searched the ground for the wayward cap. Damn it all, that was sure not the way to seduce a man, she thought, wishing she didn't have to walk past Maria's desk to get to the bathroom and a mirror.

CHAPTER 5

Ms. Stevens, this is Lucy Bettencourt. We talked about meeting for a walk-through on the Painted Lady. I need to reschedule that appointment. I have a previous engagement that I just can't cancel, but I want to make sure you know my husband and I are still very interested. We can't believe the chance to own a piece of San Francisco history is right at our fingertips. Please call me back as soon as you can, so we can reschedule. I'm looking forward to talking with you.

* * *

Stan wandered over to Peyton's desk later that afternoon. "Hey, Peyton," he said, smiling brightly at her.

Peyton looked up from her online research into the listing for the Painted Lady. "Hey, Stan," she said. She hadn't talked with him since their disastrous date. She resisted the impulse to see if Marco was listening, but she sure hoped Stan wouldn't mention the other night in front of him.

"I just got the warrant for the phone records on your case."

Wow, Devan Adams sure knew how to pull strings. "Really? That's awesome. We need her client list and a transcript of any messages she had on the phone. Did Bob Anderson bring her phone to you?"

"Yeah, he found it in her purse. She has a number of messages indicated on the call log. I'll get right on it."

"Thank you, Stan. Does she have anything on her calendar for the day she died? Appointments? Anything?"

"Let's go look. I haven't even tried to break her password yet, but it shouldn't be too hard. As soon as I got the warrant, I came over here to tell you."

Peyton rose to her feet. "I'm going to see if there's anything on Darla's phone," she told Marco. He waved a

61

hand at her without looking away from his computer screen. He'd been working on locating the owners of the Painted Lady, a couple who lived in Los Angeles. Gerald had given him the name of their lawyer and his phone number, but he was conveniently unavailable.

She followed Stan to his cubicle and waited as he squeezed past the table and slipped into his desk chair. He picked up a phone in a sparkling pink case and plugged it into something on his computer. Then his fingers flew over the keyboard and a moment later, he leaned back in his chair and smiled at her.

"Just waiting for the program to crack the password."

"You can do that?"

His smile faded. He didn't like it when she questioned his ability, but she couldn't help it. What she knew about computers could fit in a baggie.

"Sorry. I mean, I didn't know there were programs to do that."

"Yep. I got a special clearance to use this one in particular. It's very powerful."

Peyton forced a smile, glancing back down the hallway. She felt awkward, standing outside Stan's office, especially after their date.

He cleared his throat. "I'm sorry about our date the other night."

Peyton tried not to make an uncomfortable face, but talking about it was even worse than she thought. "It's okay. It wasn't your fault."

"Do men talk like that to you often?"

Peyton gave him a bewildered look. "What do you mean?"

"Comment about your…well, um…assets."

Yeah, this was just getting worse. She peered at the face of Darla's cell phone, but it didn't seem to be doing anything. "Men make comments to women all the time, Stan. Not everyone is a gentleman like you."

That made him flush with pleasure. She probably shouldn't be encouraging him.

"Do the men here talk to you like that?"

She shook her head. "They wouldn't dare. They know I'd shoot them."

"Or Marco would knock them into next Tuesday."

That made her frown. She didn't need Marco fighting her battles for her. Did he threaten people behind her back? What the hell! Her thoughts went back to this morning when he'd made Gerald Stevens sit down. She'd thought he'd done it to protect Stevens. Had he done it to protect her?

She glanced toward their desks, feeling a rush of anger. He intervened with Holmes and Anderson when she had trouble with them. In fact, if she thought about it, he was always stepping between her and some man. Shit. That was going to have to stop but quick. She wasn't having her partner protect her like she was a fragile flower. Damn it, she was tougher than he was.

"Bingo!" shouted Stan, clapping his hands and making her jump.

Peyton's attention whipped back to him. "What?" She placed a hand over her heart.

"Sorry," he said sheepishly, then he picked up the phone. "We're in."

"Pull up her calendar for me."

Stan clicked on the phone, screwing up his lips as he concentrated. "She had an appointment for today at 10:00 to show the Painted Lady. Looks like they're called the Bettencourts."

"Is there a phone number for them?"

"Yep." He grabbed a scratch pad and scribbled it down. "Nothing else for the rest of the day, but who knows what's in her messages?"

"Go back a week. Is there anything scheduled for last week?"

"Manicure on Tuesday. Meeting at the office on Wednesday. She met with the Rochesters on Monday."

"Wait, this Monday or last Monday?"

"Last Monday."

"Does it have a note about why she met with them?"

"To sign contracts. Maybe she sold a house?"

Peyton shrugged. The Rochesters must be the couple that owned the Painted Lady, the man that wanted to hire the spiritualist to cleanse the place. "Write all that down for me."

Stan did as she requested.

"Is there a number for the Rochesters?"

"Yep."

"What about a man named Dave Forrester? Does she mention him?"

Stan frowned. "It says *Dave leaves* on Tuesday."

"Add that to our list."

Stan scribbled some more and handed her the note. "I'll get a transcript of her calls to you ASAP."

"Go through the rest of her contacts and her calendar. See if she had any other appointments to show the Painted Lady."

Stan saluted. "On it!" he said brightly.

Peyton smiled and walked back to her desk.

Marco looked up as she approached. "The house is owned by the Rochesters, a couple in LA. I got a short text back from the lawyer."

"Hm, I just got their phone number. Remember, the lawyer wanted to cleanse the house."

"Right. With a spiritualist."

"Yep." Peyton sank into her desk chair. "Do you want to call them or the Bettencourts?"

"Who are the Bettencourts?"

"A couple who's supposed to look at the house at 10:00."

"I'll take the Bettencourts."

Peyton wrote the number on a pad of paper and slid it over to him. "So, not to change the subject, but do you put yourself between me and any men we encounter?"

He gave her a puzzled look. "Why do I feel like I'm walking into a trap?"

"It's just a question."

"I don't understand the question."

"When we're on a call or I have an altercation with a man at the precinct, you always step between us and try to de-escalate the situation."

"I'm still not hearing a question." His blue eyes narrowed.

Peyton exhaled in frustration. "Do you try to protect me from confrontations with men?"

Marco didn't answer for a moment, but it was enough. She knew what the answer would be. Still, she wanted him to admit it, wanted him to realize how sexist that was. She could handle herself. She'd been doing it her whole life. Her father hadn't raised a shrinking violet.

"Marco?"

"Now I know I'm walking into a trap. How about some coffee?"

"How about you answer me?"

"We're partners, Brooks. That's what partners do."

"I don't step between you and people."

"Well," he said, holding out his hand.

"Well?" An edge crept into her voice.

"Please let this go," he pleaded. "Where is this coming from anyway?"

"Stan said you'd knock a guy into next Tuesday if he made an inappropriate comment about my..." She hesitated. She might be giving too much away.

"About your what?"

"Forget it," she said, reaching for her phone.

"Brooks, about your what?"

She blew out air. "My ass, okay?"

He half-rose out of his chair. "Did someone in this precinct make a comment about your ass?"

"Forget it, all right."

"Brooks!"

"No, it was hypothetical." She focused on the Rochesters' number. "Let's get back to the case."

He settled back in his chair, but she could feel his eyes searching her. She didn't meet his gaze. She should never have brought this up. What the hell was she thinking? She knew he got protective over her, looked out for her. He was just protecting her back the way she protected his. That's what partners did.

She dialed the Rochesters. After a few rings, a man answered the phone. "Hello?" he said.

"Mr. Rochester, this is Inspector Peyton Brooks of the SFPD."

"Inspector, I'm glad you called. I've been meaning to call you. My lawyer talked with Gerald Stevens this morning and we're devastated to learn there was such an unfortunate accident in our home."

"Mr. Rochester…"

"Samuel, please."

"Samuel, I know your lawyer talked with Gerald. We were there when he took his call."

"Inspector Brooks, when do you think the house will be released? We need to be able to show it and this isn't helping anything. My wife and I are worried people won't want to buy it now that it's been the scene of a murder. Do you have any suspects?"

"Samuel…"

"The quicker this case gets solved the better. You don't think someone killed Darla because of the house, do you?"

Peyton stared at the phone. "What? Why would someone kill her because of the house?"

"Because it's a piece of San Francisco history. What if the murderer wants notoriety? You know, to become famous as a result of his crime. Like the Zodiac Killer or something. You know, the Painted Lady Killer?"

That gave Peyton pause. She didn't like the fact that this guy took a souvenir from the crime scene. Could the location have been more important than the woman? She made a note on her pad.

"In Darla's phone calendar, it says she met with you last Monday to sign the contracts."

"Yes, we met in her office."

"I have to ask this, Samuel. Where were you and your wife two days ago?"

"We were here, Inspector. In fact, we had some work done on our car. I can forward you the receipt and I believe they have a video camera in the repair shop. You could call them for the surveillance tape, right?"

"Right. Please send me the receipt and also the receipt for your flight the Monday before last. I just have to cross off any leads I might have."

"Of course. Just text me a fax number and I'll fax it to you as soon as I can. I want this case solved. Every day that it goes unsolved means money down the drain."

"And a woman who doesn't get justice, Samuel," she scolded mildly.

"Yes, of course that, but you have to understand, we need the capital from the house to build our business. We're opening up an antique store, Inspector Brooks. Soon we'll have an online presence and you can buy directly from us there. We ship anywhere."

Peyton rolled her eyes. Sure, she collected antiques, but most people would call it junk, garage sale junk. "Thanks, Samuel. Look, I need to go. Fax those receipts over as soon as you can."

"Right away. Goodbye, Inspector."

"Goodbye, Samuel." She hung up and looked over at Marco. "He wants me to buy his antiques."

"Really?" Marco gave a laugh, leaning back in his chair. "I didn't know you were into antiques."

"Didn't you know the furniture in my house is antique?"

"That's what you're calling it now?"

"It's better than junk."

He rose to his feet. "How about I buy you a cup of coffee, Mrs. Rockefeller, and you can tell me all about it."

She pushed back her chair and followed him into the break room. "How did your conversation with the Bettencourts go?"

"Mrs. Bettencourt was distraught that Darla died in the house. She wanted to know if the blood stains would come out."

"Dear God," Peyton said, grimacing. "What is wrong with these people? A woman was murdered."

Marco reached for the coffee pot and a mug. "They sure don't think like normal people. And these names – Rochester, Bettencourt – it's like a guide book to the 1%." He slid the mug over to Peyton.

She reached for the sugar and began shaking it into her coffee. "So I'm leaning more and more towards a rivalry, D'Angelo. I think we can cross off the Bettencourts and the Rochesters and even Gerald Stevens. I just don't like him for the doer."

"So, Jules is it?"

"And Lori Hardy." She added another couple of shakes, then reached for a spoon and the milk, adding a splash of it to the cup.

"The woman who found her?"

"Yeah. I mean they were in direct competition with each other." Setting the spoon down, she reached for the sugar again and shook it a few more times. She felt Marco watching her and looked up.

He leaned against the counter, lifting his mug to his lips. "Why don't you get a cup of sugar and darken it with a splash of coffee?"

"Leave me alone," she said, giving the shaker one more shake for good measure and glaring at him. Of course he took his coffee black, and he was a vegetarian, and he worked out in the gym...everyday. Well, she ran. Sometimes.

Lifting her mug, she walked over to the table and took a seat. A box of donuts sat in the middle of the table and her fingers itched to grab one. He sat down across from her, forcing her to look away from the tempting treat.

"Lori Hardy had nearly as much to gain as Darla if she sold the house to those yuppie kids," said Marco, curling his fingers around his mug.

"You mean the Coxs? I guess she did." She thought about it for a moment. Why would Lori kill Darla, then bring the Coxs into the house on the pretense of showing it, only to discover the body? Maybe she wanted an alibi. It was a pretty cagey plot, actually. "I can make a scenario where that might benefit her. What if she thought that the Rochesters might sign with her after Darla's death, since she was bringing a potential client to the house?"

Marco made a face. "It's got a lot of holes, Brooks."

"Okay, how do you think it went down?"

"I honestly don't know. I know Abe said the attacker wouldn't have to be much bigger than Darla if he or she got the drop on her, but it takes a lot of upper body strength to strangle someone. And why would a rival take her scarf?"

"Victory over an adversary or maybe it was just a pretty scarf."

"You mean the killer might be wearing it?" He gave a shiver.

Peyton started to respond, but Bob Anderson appeared in the doorway, holding a folded set of papers. "Here's your warrants for Darla Stevens' office." He handed them to Marco, refusing to look at Peyton.

"Thank you, Bob," Peyton said in a syrupy voice. "I surely do appreciate it."

He gave her a disgusted look and turned away.

Marco tapped the papers on the table. "Did he say something about your ass?" he demanded.

For a moment, Peyton forgot what he was talking about, then it came to her and she barked out a laugh. "God no! He hates me."

Marco rose to his feet and leaned over her, staring down into her eyes. "That doesn't mean he can't notice your ass, Brooks," he said, then turned and walked out of the room.

Peyton's attention went back to the box of donuts. With a huff of exasperation, she grabbed a napkin and snatched one out of the box. It was covered in chocolate with pink sprinkles on top, just the way she loved it. Taking a bite, she hurried after her partner, stopping by her desk to snag her leather jacket on the way toward the front of the precinct.

* * *

The Bay City Properties offices was modern and elegant, much like Gerald Stevens' condo. The reception room had highly polished wood floors and black leather chairs without arms. A few end tables in lacquered black paint held neatly stacked magazines, mostly about home improvement or model homes.

A young receptionist, with an hourglass figure poured into a midnight blue sheath dress and six-inch screw-me pumps, greeted them. Her white blond hair was pulled back into a tight ponytail and her lashes looked like two caterpillars stuck to her eyelids. Black mascara winged away from her unnaturally purple eyes.

She gave Marco a sultry smile, ignoring Peyton altogether. Peyton slapped her badge down on the glass counter, along with the warrants. "Inspector Peyton Brooks and Marco D'Angelo from the SFPD."

The receptionist rose to her feet. She had to be nearly six feet tall in those pumps. Peyton hated having to look up at her. "Gerald said you'd be coming in. He's not here." She turned, so she had to look over one shoulder, *a totally natural pose*, Peyton thought. She had one of those little girl voices, designed to make men come to heel. "He's so distraught."

"Distraught? Wow, that's a big word," said Peyton.

That didn't even earn her a glare. As far as Real Estate Barbie was concerned, Peyton wasn't even in the room. She looked up at her partner. Marco was giving the receptionist his sexiest smile.

Peyton motioned to the hallway beyond the counter. "Should we just go back? I'm sure Darla's office is labeled."

Real Estate Barbie turned, giving Marco a view of her other side. "I think I'm supposed to ask for a warrant, aren't I?"

"Yeah," Marco said. "It's always a good idea."

She giggled.

Peyton picked up the paper and waved it at her. "Warrant?"

"I'll show you her office," she said without even looking at the papers. "Follow me."

Peyton briefly closed her eyes for patience, then followed Real Estate Barbie's swaying hips around the counter, Marco on her heels. It always amazed Peyton that her partner could be so intelligent and clever on a case, but the minute a pretty woman batted her eyes at him and started talking in a little girl voice, all those brains migrated south. Marco was no better than any other man when there was a woman in heat.

"Gerald told you he's staying home today?"

"He has to make the funeral arrangements," she said, pursing her lips into a pout. "Gerald was all Darla had, well except for her sister – no children, no parents." She paused at a frosted glass door with Darla's name etched in gold on the outside. "Isn't that the saddest thing you've ever heard?"

It was pretty sad, Peyton thought. Although she wasn't necessarily in a better position. Except for her mother, no one else in the world would be around to make her funeral arrangements. Well, except Abe. Abe would make them, but he'd probably have her buried in a fur-lined hot-pink casket.

"Her sister isn't helping with the arrangements?" Peyton asked.

"I don't know. She and Gerald didn't get along, so Darla didn't get to see her much." Real Estate Barbie opened the door and waved them inside. "I'll just let you get to it. If you need anything," and here she batted those eyelashes at Marco, "I'll be at my desk."

"Thank you," he said gruffly.

Peyton stepped into the office. Darla had a number of black leather chairs arranged before a black lacquered desk. A silver laptop lay on the top of the desk and behind it was a number of black file cabinets. Her window was draped in white sheers and looked out over the alley between the building next to them. Except for the laptop, there was nothing else on the desk, not even a picture frame or any personal effects.

Peyton went around the desk and took a seat, opening the laptop. She pressed the on-button as Marco wandered over to open the file cabinets. As she waited for the computer to boot up, she opened Darla's desk drawers. In the top drawer, she found a leather-bound notebook. *Damn, these people liked their cowhide.* Pulling it out, she found it was a notebook for clients – brief descriptions of what they looked like, what they enjoyed (chocolate, champagne, cigars), and what sort of house they were looking to buy. At the back of it, she had an index card taped to the inside cover with her passwords listed. Older ones were crossed off.

At the start screen, Peyton pressed a D for Darla. The user name *dstevens* popped up, so Peyton went with that, then used the latest password to access her laptop. A moment later she was in. She smiled to herself, feeling very Stan Neumanish. She found a file that said *Clients* on it and she opened it. They were helpfully arranged by date. She saw the Rochesters name, but the rest of the entries had a closing date. Peyton assumed that meant the houses had closed escrow.

"You got in?" said Marco, coming to stand behind her chair.

"Yep. This is her client list. It looks like the Painted Lady was the only thing she was currently working on."

Marco leaned over her shoulder and she could smell the sandalwood of his cologne. Damn the man smelled good.

She forced her attention back to the laptop. "These are people whose houses she's sold?" he asked.

"Yeah."

"Better print that out, Brooks. We might have to go back over all the clients, find out if anyone was disgruntled."

Peyton grimaced. "That's a whole lot of clients, D'Angelo."

"Yeah, well, you got a better idea?"

Peyton thought for a moment, then she hit print. "Nope." She could hear the printer working under the desk and she reached down into the small space and extracted the papers, tapping them together on the desktop, then she opened the drawer and found a paperclip, bundling them together.

Going back to the laptop, she closed the client file and found another one that said *Potential Buyers*. This spreadsheet listed the names of the buyers, the realtor representing them (if any), the date they'd contacted Darla, and what property they were interested in. The listing was in alphabetical order and there were over a thousand names on it.

"Don't tell me we have to print this too," she whined.

"We're gonna have to get Cho and Simons to help us." Cho and Simons were the second, more experienced detective team in their precinct. They were not going to like this chore, not one little bit.

Peyton tapped her fingers on the desk, studying the sheet. "Some of these entries are really old, D'Angelo, like six or seven years. Don't you think we can eliminate those?"

"Maybe at first." He straightened and she looked up at him. His eyes were still fixed on the list. "I mean, we can start with her most recent contacts. Can't you sort a spreadsheet by date?"

Peyton glanced back at it, chewing her inner lip. She was pretty sure you could, but she wasn't sure she remembered how. However, she didn't want to call Stan for something this trivial. "Any ideas how?"

"I think you click at the top of the row you want to sort by. Try it. What could it hurt?"

Peyton slid the cursor to the row she wanted and clicked, praying she wouldn't mess up this important data. "Okay, that's the older ones on top now. I think if I click again, it'll show me the newer ones, right?"

"You know more than I do, Brooks," he said, leaning on the top of the desk chair with both arms.

Peyton clicked again, then clapped when the newest dates sprang to the top. Then she scrolled down, feeling her happiness dissipate. There were still at least thirty new contacts over the last month. "Man, this woman knew how to network. Look at this. All these contacts are in the past month." She pointed at one in particular. "Here are the Bettencourts and the Coxs. It lists Lori Hardy as the Coxs' realtor. The Evans, the Grosvenors...ha, look at this one, Tom Jefferson. Seriously?"

Marco laughed. "Print it out. We still need to check in with Jules and get her alibi and we need to see if we can talk to the people Gerald Stevens was apparently meeting with when Darla went to the big house."

Peyton printed the list and logged off Darla's computer. "Went to the big house? Are you serious, D'Angelo?"

He moved around the desk, dropping into one of the leather chairs. "I'm trying to be respectful of the woman's demise, Brooks."

"Yeah, but that's a little cheesy, don't you think?"

He shifted on the chair, the leather creaking. "This is uncomfortable."

"Yeah, well, imagine how uncomfortable it was for the cow," she said, tapping her new stack into place and paper clipping it.

"Thanks, Brooks, that's just the sort of image any vegetarian wants in his head."

She shrugged. "Just trying to be respectful of the cow's demise, D'Angelo," she said, giving him a wicked smile.

CHAPTER 6

Darla, it's Deb again. I tried to call Gerald, but he won't answer the phone. He's such an ass. I'll never understand why you married him. Look, I get he hates me. I know he blames me for the divorce, but I'm really worried about you. Couldn't the rat bastard at least text me and let me know you're all right? It's like he takes pleasure in torturing me. Darla, please call me back. I'm starting to panic.

* * *

Peyton and Marco closed Darla's office door and walked out to the reception area. Real Estate Barbie was back at her post, reading a magazine. She looked up as they appeared beside her. "Find anything?"

Peyton held up the two packets of papers. "We got her contact list. We're gonna run down some names."

"Oh, good. I sure hope you find out who did this." She leaned forward and Peyton was gifted with the knowledge that she wore a lacy, black bra. So was Marco and he didn't bother to look away. "I was thinking of becoming a real estate agent myself." She gave a delicate shiver. "Just think. It could have been me in that garage."

"Right," said Peyton. "Look, um, sorry, I don't know your name."

"January."

"Sorry? January?"

"January Applegate. Here's the funny thing. I was born in April." She giggled.

Marco made a soft chuckling sound. Peyton glared over her shoulder at him.

"Yeah, that's funny," Peyton said, looking back at January. "Look, January, has anyone called into the office lately wanting to file a complaint on one of the realtors?"

"A complaint?"

"Yeah, a complaint. A client that wasn't happy or any other call from someone who was upset."

"Oh, you mean mad," she said in her little girl's voice.

"Right, someone mad."

"Not that I remember."

"What happens if someone calls in mad?"

January picked up a notepad. "I write it on here and give it to Gerald."

"When was the last time you wrote a note to Gerald about a mad client?"

January opened the cover on the notepad and Peyton could see it was printed on NCR paper. Flipping back a few pages, January inspected the faint writing on the notes. "Um, the last complaint was…" She looked up and her lips moved as she counted back. "Five months ago."

"Was the complaint against Darla?" asked Peyton.

"Nope. It was against Eleanor." She leaned forward again, dropping her voice. "She talked the client out of taking a deal he really wanted to take, then the guy had to settle for a much lower price. I remember that one. Man, that guy was heated."

Marco reached for his phone. "Can I take a picture of that, January?"

"Of course," she said, handing him the notepad.

He smiled at her and backed up, bracing the notepad on the desk behind Peyton. She could hear him rifling through the pages, double checking what Real Estate Barbie had told them. She focused her attention on January.

"Gerald said he was in a meeting on the day Darla died. He was meeting with two of his agents to discuss a condo complex that's opening in Emeryville."

"Right. Bayview Arms."

"Bayview Arms?" Peyton repeated. "Do you remember who he was meeting with?"

"Um." January considered, tapping a long, painted nail against her lower lip. "That would have been Sarah and Tyesha."

"Do you remember how long that meeting lasted?"

"Well, I took them coffee about 4:00."

"And you saw Gerald there?"

"Of course I did, silly. He asked me to order his dinner for delivery, so I called the Peking Palace. Gerald loves his General's chicken. I keep telling him that it'll put on weight, but he doesn't care. I must order from Peking Palace at least three times a week." She leaned over and opened a desk drawer, pulling out a folder. "I have the receipt here. Gerald has me keep all of these for his taxes." She began searching through the receipts in the folder. "Here it is. One order of General's chicken and steamed rice." She passed the receipt to Peyton.

Peyton looked at it. It was dated the day Darla died and someone had written the delivery time on the top. 4:45. She passed it to Marco, so he could take a picture of it with his phone.

"January, do you know if any of the other realtors in this office were upset by Darla's success?"

"No, why would they be? They all do so well for themselves."

"Maybe because she was married to the boss?"

January sighed. "No, Eleanor's married and Tyesha's engaged." She lowered her voice. "I think Sarah might be a lesbian. She gives me funny looks."

Yeah, that must mean she's a lesbian, thought Peyton in annoyance.

"I've never heard anything and trust me, I hear everything. I know exactly who's sleeping with who and who they want to sleep with."

Peyton had to admit that Real Estate Barbie was more savvy that she'd thought. "Do you know Jules Walters?"

"Darla's friend? Yeah, Jules works in this building. She's awesome. She's so pretty and she's always so nice to me."

"Did she and Darla ever fight?"

"Are you kidding? The only person I ever saw Darla fight with was Gerald. Darla had no enemies. None. Everyone loved her."

Someone hadn't loved her. Someone had wanted her dead.

"Thank you, January." Peyton gave her a business card. "If you think of anything, will you call me?"

"Sure."

Marco handed her back the notepad and receipt.

"Good luck, Inspectors," she said as they headed for the door.

* * *

"Well, check off Gerald Stevens from our suspect list," said Peyton, pausing in the hallway outside the office. "Damn it, I wouldn't have minded locking that arrogant bastard up."

"Being arrogant and being a murderer are two very different things, Brooks."

"Yeah, but now we have to figure this out and I was hoping we could just put this one to bed."

"I'm still liking your rivalry angle," he said, nudging her toward the elevator with his shoulder. "What's say we talk to Jules again?"

"Sounds like a plan," she said, "but afterward, I want lunch."

"Okay. Where do you want to go?"

"Peking Palace. I think we should try the General's chicken."

"Vegetarian, Brooks."

"Then I should try it. General's chicken's sweet, right?"

78

"How would I know?" He pressed the elevator button. "Any idea what floor Jules is on?"

"Third," she said.

The elevator opened and they stepped inside.

"Maybe they have General's tofu?" she suggested.

Marco gave her a patient smile. "We'll go to Peking Palace after this. I'll find something I can eat."

"Don't make it sound like you're sacrificing something, D'Angelo. It's not my fault you're a crunchy granola guy."

"I'm not a crunchy granola guy. I just don't like eating flesh."

Peyton gave a long-suffering sigh. "Do you always have to make it sound so disgusting?"

"I'm not the one eating the stuff, Brooks." The elevator door opened and they stepped out. They found Jules' office and pushed open the door, surprised to find Jules herself sitting behind the reception desk.

She rose to her feet at their entrance. She didn't look as pressed and polished as she had at Darla's house. In fact, her makeup was smudged and her hair was pulled up in a messy ponytail. Her skirt had wrinkles in it and she wore flats.

"Inspectors? Do you have any information?" she asked them, clasping her hands near her breast.

"We're working on a few angles, crossing off a few things," said Peyton, glancing around the room. It looked very similar to the one Gerald Stevens had downstairs. "Jules, I thought you were a realtor?"

"I am. I'm just filling in for Karen while she's at lunch." She drew a deep breath. "I didn't feel like going out."

"I understand." Peyton shifted weight. She felt guilty asking this of her, especially seeing how upset she seemed to be, but she might be upset because she'd strangled her best friend. Peyton wouldn't know until they checked Jules' alibi. "I'm sorry I have to ask you this, but can you tell me where you were the afternoon Darla died? We need to cover the hours between 1:00 and 3:00."

Jules stared at Peyton without speaking, then her eyes lifted to Marco. Peyton held her breath. Were they about to get a surprise confession? Stranger things had happened, but Peyton wasn't usually this lucky. Still, it had to happen at some point in her career, right?

"I was here. I told you I got that listing on Mason. I was writing up the contract that afternoon to take it to the buyer at 5:00, then I was going to meet Darla afterward to celebrate with drinks."

"How long does it usually take to write up a contract?"

"For a seven-million-dollar house? Hours. I had to write a marketing plan and I had to research comps. There aren't many comps in that price range, so it's pretty involved. I even cold called some of my clients to find out if they were interested."

"You made those calls on your cell phone?"

"Yes. Can't you get the records and won't it show where I was when I made them?"

"Yes, it will. Was anyone else in the office during that time?"

"My broker, Joanne. She was helping me go over the offer. I think we met about 2:30."

"Is Joanne in now?"

"No, she's out, but…" Jules grabbed a business card and passed it to Peyton. "Here's her direct number." Then her eyes widened. "Also, they have a camera in the front lobby of the building. I'll bet they have me leaving at 4:30 to meet with the client."

Peyton couldn't deny a small measure of disappointment. It would have been so much easier if Jules had just confessed, but Peyton didn't like her for the doer. The problem was Peyton didn't like any of their suspects for the doer. This damn case was going to be harder to solve than she'd thought. Still, she smiled at the realtor and held up the card.

"We'll give Joanne a call and clear this up. I appreciate you being so cooperative."

"I want Darla's murderer caught, Inspector Brooks."

"So do we, Jules. You take care of yourself until we do, okay?"

Jules nodded and they turned to leave.

Once on the other side of the door, Peyton sighed. "Now I really need General's chicken."

Marco chuckled. "You just found out about it today. How can you need it?"

"I didn't just find out about it. I've always known about it. I just forgot it exists."

"I see," said Marco, draping an arm around her shoulders. "You just want something sweet, that's all this is."

She bumped him with her shoulder. "And this surprises you why?"

*　*　*

After they grabbed lunch at Peking Palace, they headed back to the precinct. Maria was sitting at her desk when they entered and her face lit up when she saw Marco. Marco pretended to tip an imaginary hat at her.

"Hey, Maria," he said.

"Hey, Marco baby," she purred at him. "How's the case going?"

"Frustrating," he answered.

Peyton moved around his six foot four frame. "Is Defino in her office?"

Maria's face twisted into a scowl. "No, she's having lunch with the mayor."

Peyton frowned. "Lunch with the mayor?"

"He wants to start some task force on crime. What do I know, Brooks?" Maria leaned back in her chair. "Maybe you wanna try solving a crime once in a while."

"And maybe you wanna get me some coffee, so I can solve it?"

"I'm not your servant, Brooks. Get your own damn coffee and lay off the sugar or your ass is gonna be as big as a hot air balloon."

Peyton started toward her, but Marco laid a hand on her shoulder. "Go update the whiteboard in the conference room," he told her, turning her toward the conference room door. "I'll get the coffee."

Peyton glared at Maria, but she let herself be directed to the door. "And see if there's any left over cake. That'll work better than coffee to give me my hot air balloon ass."

Marco shook his head and started toward the break room. "Every freakin' day," he muttered under his breath.

Peyton took off her leather jacket as she entered the room and tossed it on the table, then she grabbed the white erase marker off the rolling board and studied their list of suspects. She crossed off Gerald Stevens and Jules Walters. She studied Debra Lawrence's name.

January said Gerald was making all the funeral arrangements, but Peyton found it hard to believe her sister wouldn't want to be in on this. She needed to see if Stan could pull the sister's phone number off Darla's phone. She wondered if Debra even knew her sister was dead, despite what Gerald had said.

Her cell phone rang and Peyton reached for it without looking at the display. She thumbed it on, feeling defeated by their lack of leads. Only two suspects remained, if she ignored the list of clients and potential buyers. God, this case was frustrating.

"Hello?" she said into the phone.

"Hey, little soul sista," came Abe's booming voice through the line. "What's say you, me and that gorgeous hunk of man you call a partner hook up for dinner tonight?"

"Sounds good. Where do you want to go?"

"What are you in the mood for? I'm wanting tempura. What's say we go to Japantown?"

"We had Chinese for lunch. Can we do something else?"

"Chinese and Japanese are not the same things, toots, but I hear you. Okay, what about seafood?"

"Seafood? Where?"

"*Alioto's?*"

"*Alioto's?* On the Wharf? Tonight? God, Abe, Marco's gonna hate that. So many tourists."

"We'll have a lovely view of the bay and the Golden Gate. I haven't eaten at *Alioto's* in years, Peyton. Humor me. I'll let you pick the next three places. It'll be fun pretending to be a tourist."

"It won't be fun. It'll be crowded."

"Please," Abe begged. "I'll drive."

"No way is Marco going to get into your Mini, Abe, and you know that. We'll drive. Meet us here at 6:00."

"Okey dokey!" he said happily.

She looked up as Marco stepped into the room, carrying two cups of coffee. "Abe's coming here at 6:00 and we're going to dinner."

Marco hesitated, looking like he might bolt. "Where?"

"It's a surprise," she said brightly, moving to take the mug from his hand. "Sugar?"

"An entire cane," he mocked.

She took a sip. He knew exactly how to make her coffee for her. "Okay, Abe, see you then."

"Bye, toots." And he was off.

Marco sank into a chair at the head of the table, sipping his own coffee. "Where are we going to dinner?"

"*Alioto's,*" she said, turning her back on him before he could say anything.

"*Alioto's?* Brooks, that's on the Wharf."

"Is it? I wasn't sure."

She could feel Marco's eyes boring daggers into her back. Sure, it was a weak lie. Everyone knew where *Alioto's* was, but Peyton didn't want to argue with him.

"It'll be crowded with tourists and the parking's a bitch."

"Abe's gonna drive us in the Mini," she said, knowing that would divert his attention from the Wharf.

"Oh, hell no! I'm not riding in that ridiculous clown car."

"Then we'll take the Charger." She turned and smiled at him, picking up her marker again.

He narrowed his eyes on her. "You just played me, didn't you?"

She gave him her most innocent look. "How?"

"You threw up something more distasteful than the Wharf, so the Wharf would be reasonable."

She shook her head, widening her eyes. "That's manipulative and I would never be manipulative with you, Marco."

He leaned back in his chair, lifting his coffee mug. "All right," he said slowly. "All right. I'll remember this when it comes time to write the report on this case."

Peyton made a scoffing sound and turned back to the board. She always wrote the reports, always. He pretended to have dyslexia, so he could get out of it, but she'd let him have his way. If he thought he was gaining something by making her write a report she was already going to write, so be it.

"Our suspect list is down to two."

He made a noncommittal sound. "Looking pretty slim. I'll bet we're going to have to go through both of those lists name by name."

Peyton tilted back her head and groaned. "That's gonna take years."

"Weeks, yep. Weeks." He sighed. "You wanna take the boyfriend or the sister."

"I'll take the sister. I think I can get a number from Stan. We probably need to pay the sister a home visit. I'm not sure she's even been notified yet."

Marco pushed himself to his feet. "God, I hate that. If you think that, then we better leave that for the morning."

Peyton nodded. "Can you call Gerald and confirm he talked to the sister?"

"Yeah, I'll do that before I put a call in to David." He walked out of the room.

Peyton added the two lists they'd taken from Darla's computer to the board, then recapped the pen, picked up her coffee and leather jacket, and left the room, ignoring Maria as she went past. She set the coffee on her desk, tossed her jacket over her chair, and headed toward Stan's office.

Stan beamed at her behind his coke bottle glasses. He wore a collared shirt over his t-shirt, jeans, and his ubiquitous Converse sneakers. The t-shirt said *Are you the Death Star? Because you blow me away.*

"Funny," she said, pointing at it.

He looked down, smoothing his hands over his chest. "You get it?"

"Sure." She smiled at him. "Did you get the messages off Darla Steven's phone?"

Stan wheeled backward to a table along his back wall, picking up a couple sheets of paper. "Here's what I could find. Nothing too incriminating, if you ask me. I also pulled her call list for the last month." He showed her a list of phone numbers. "Nothing jumps out here either. I could link all these numbers with people she interacted with often. I highlighted those in yellow. That would be her ex-husband, her friend Jules, her sister Debra, and the office landline."

Peyton pointed to the one number that appeared nearly every week. "Is this her sister?"

"Yep."

"What are the pink highlights?"

"I think those must be clients. They show up frequently. This is the Bettencourts and this is the Rochesters, see?"

"Right. Can we identify the other numbers in pink?"

"Only if we call them directly. She didn't have them listed by names in her contacts. That's how I connected the Bettencourts and Rochesters. I used the numbers you and Marco called."

Peyton glanced at the messages. "You transcribed these for me?"

"Me and Maria. She types faster than I do."

Peyton smiled at him. "Thank you, Stan."

He beamed at her. "Anytime, Peyton," he said.

Peyton headed back to her desk and found Marco ending a call. Peyton set the papers on her blotter and leaned against her chair. "Was that Gerald?"

Marco nodded. "He said he left a message for Debra about her sister."

"What? He didn't go talk to her in person?"

"Nope."

"What a bastard!"

Marco slid a piece of paper over to Peyton's side of the desk. "Here's the sister's number. You get to call her and tell her we want to come out and talk to her."

Peyton sighed. "You give me the shit duty. You know that, D'Angelo?"

"*Alioto's* on the Wharf, Brooks. That's all I gotta say. *Alioto's* on the Wharf."

Peyton knew she'd been had. She leaned over and picked up the message. "Fine."

*　*　*

Alioto's on *Fisherman's Wharf* opened in 1925. Run by three generations of Aliotos, it was famous for its view of the bay and its traditional Sicilian cuisine. Peyton loved its garlic bread – real garlic and melted butter poured over San Francisco sour dough. Heaven.

The entrance to the restaurant was right on the Wharf. Steel drums and street performers plied their trade along the walkways, attracting tourists. Seafood restaurants placed chairs and tables outside under tin-roof awnings and the smells of the ocean and garlic mingled to make Peyton's stomach growl.

She threaded her way through the crowd behind
Marco and Abe. Since both men were over six feet, they cut a
path through the tourist crowd with ease. At the door, Abe
leaned close to the young maître d' and passed him a folded
bill. Peyton didn't even want to know how much Abe gave
the guy. It was sure a hell of a lot more than Peyton could
afford.

The young man motioned them up the stairs and into
the restaurant where he seated them before the windows
overlooking the bay. The setting sun filtered through the
shades, bathing the entire room in a rosy light.

Crisp white tablecloths covered the table with bright
blue napkins set at equally spaced intervals. More silverware
than Peyton knew what to do with sat beside the white china
plates. She glanced around, wondering if her jeans, leather
jacket, and kick-ass boots were out of place, but most people
wore nearly the same thing. California casual. Peyton loved it.

As soon as they sat, a waiter appeared, wearing a blue
apron around his waist with a starched collared shirt and a
black tie. He passed them all menus and clasped his hands
before him. A busboy poured water into their glasses and
placed a loaf of garlic bread in the middle of the table. Peyton
immediately reached for a piece, setting it on her bread plate.

"Can I start you off with a drink?" asked the waiter as
the busboy retreated.

"It's gotta be a martini for me," said Abe, placing his
long fingered hand against his chest.

"Very good, sir. What kind?"

Abe glanced at Peyton. "Make it chocolate. What do
you say, sweets? You gonna join me in one?"

Alioto's was famous for its martinis. The martini came
in a martini glass with chocolate swirls around the inside and
a chocolate kiss attached to a swizzle stick and garnished with
chocolate shavings. Staring at the picture in the menu, Peyton
didn't feel that adventurous.

Besides, they had to get up early in the morning and
try to track Darla's sister down. Peyton had called her, but

she'd gotten her voice mail and she hadn't wanted to leave a message of this magnitude for her.

"I think I'll pass on that one, Abe. I'll take whatever beer you have on tap."

"Very good, ma'am." The waiter turned to Marco. "And you, sir?"

"Bring me the same as her," he grumbled, reaching for the bread.

Peyton and Abe offered the waiter a commiserate smile and he gave a brief nod before he headed toward the kitchen.

"So, how's the case going?" asked Abe. He wore a lime-green silk shirt with brown swirls all over it and darker green slacks. He had green suede loafers on his feet and green beads threaded through his dreadlocks.

In San Francisco, you could always tell the tourists from the locals. A pink elephant in a tutu could waltz down the Embarcadero and a local wouldn't give it a second look, but the tourist would wrench his neck trying to get a peek. Just so with Abe. Not a single local gave the six-foot-tall black man in dreadlocks and Mardi Gras get-up a second look, but the tourists nearly smashed into each other as they passed by. Peyton loved going out in public with Abe. It always felt like a celebration.

"Our suspect list is either two or two hundred people long. We just don't know."

"Huh," said Abe, considering. "Well, that *is* frustrating."

"Yep. And tomorrow we need to talk to one of the suspects – her sister who inherited everything Darla had. The ex-husband let the sister know she was dead by voice message."

"Cold blooded bastard. You sure he's not the doer?"

Marco tore a piece of garlic bread in half. "He's got an alibi," he said, popping one half in his mouth.

Abe gave him a flirtatious smile. "Nothing like seeing a sexy Italian eating the food of his home country," he said, winking at Marco.

Marco huffed and looked out the window, shoving the other half of the bread in his mouth.

Peyton hid her own smile behind her menu as the waiter returned with their drinks. She couldn't deny, Abe's drink looked a lot more fun than hers and Marco's.

"Can I take your order?"

Peyton went back to studying the menu. There were so many choices and she knew she'd never get Marco to come back out here again anytime soon. She really needed to get a boyfriend who could spoil her, she thought.

In the end, Peyton ordered the *Risotto Nonna Rose* with bay shrimp, crab legs, peas and mushrooms. Marco got the baked manicotti with ricotta and spinach, but Abe insisted on the lobster. At market rate prices, Peyton knew her cop paycheck couldn't afford that.

"Very good," said the waiter, collecting their menus and walking away.

Abe curled his fingers around his martini glass. "So, who are the two suspects left on the list?"

"Her new boyfriend, David Forrester, and her sister Debra Lawrence," said Peyton. "Marco tried to reach David, but a woman answered. She identified herself as his wife."

"Well, there's motive, then."

"Except the boyfriend was on a plane at the time Darla got herself strangled," said Marco. "He faxed the plane ticket to Maria and Stan's going to verify it with the flight manifest."

"So he's still a suspect until Stan gets the manifest?" asked Abe.

"Technically, but I don't like him for the doer," said Peyton. "Even though he was cheating on his wife, the wife didn't know about it, so he had no reason to kill Darla."

"Unless she was threatening to tell his wife?"

Peyton made a face and took a sip of her beer. "Jules, her best friend, doesn't even think she knew he was married."

"So the sister then?"

"That's all we got left," said Peyton. "I really thought I had something with the rivalry."

"What do you mean?" asked Abe, smacking his lips over his martini.

"These women sell these high end houses. They're in competition to see who can get the biggest listing. What if Darla stole the Painted Lady out from under another agent?"

"Yeah, but to kill someone over that?" said Abe. "I don't know, that seems thin."

Peyton nodded. "I know."

"What about a disgruntled client?"

"Gerald didn't mention anyone and Stan transcribed her phone messages for me. She had no threatening messages. We asked January about complaints and…"

"January?" asked Abe.

"The receptionist for Gerald Stevens."

"January. How do you like that?" He slapped Marco with the back of his hand. "We could adopt a little overseas baby and name it November."

Marco glared at him. "No, we can't."

Abe laughed and waved him off. "I'm gonna wear you down one of these days, Angel."

"No, you're not," he said, then he gulped his beer.

Abe laughed again, undaunted. "Go on, toots. You asked January about complaints?"

"And she said there were none against Darla."

"Hm, no threatening messages, no rivalries, no complaints. What you have, darlin', is a whole lot of nothing."

Peyton hung her head. She knew it. They were going to have to go through that list, that long, long lists of clients.

Abe picked up his drink, holding it against the light coming through the bay windows. "Unless you're looking in the wrong place."

Peyton glared at him. Of course they were looking in the wrong place. She knew that, she didn't need Abe to tell her that. She needed someone to point them in the right direction and fast, because...she felt a drop in her stomach...because she just knew this wasn't going to be the last kill.

CHAPTER 7

Ms. Stevens, I got your number from an ad in the Home section of the Examiner. You recently sold a condo in Gramercy Towers for 1.5 mil. I'm looking for a single family home because I need a garage. I collect vintage cars and I like to work on them, so I need a property that can handle my hobby. You should know, Ms. Stevens, that I'll be paying in cash. I just recently got an inheritance, a significant inheritance, and I'm looking to make a purchase sooner rather than later. I'll text you my number. Please call.

* * *

Peyton grabbed a coffee mug and filled it, then grabbed the sugar dispenser and poured directly into the mug.

"You better hope you never get diabetes, baby girl," came Frank Smith's voice in the doorway. He walked around her and grabbed his own mug.

Peyton reached for a spoon and stirred the coffee. No one else in the precinct would dare call her *baby girl*, but Frank had always taken on a fatherly role with her and she liked him. "I add that to my nightly prayers, Frank," she said, facing him and reaching up to straighten his tie.

He poured his own coffee as she fussed with his tie clasp. "Where's that hulk of a partner of yours?"

"Getting us something for breakfast." She patted the tie in place and reached for her coffee. Before she could say anything else, Maria's voice came over the intercom.

"Brooks, you got a visitor here."

Peyton sighed, taking a sip of the coffee. "Better get right on that."

"She gets snippy if you don't."

"She gets snippy if I do," Peyton said, heading for the door.

Smith's laugh trailed after her.

Dropping her coffee off at her desk, she moved toward the front of the precinct. Maria turned to face her from the counter where she'd been talking to a woman with brown hair, brown eyes, wearing a pair of jeans and an oversized sweater.

"This is Debra Lawrence, Brooks. Darla Stevens' sister."

Peyton's steps faltered and she drew a deep breath, then she held out her hand. "Nice to meet you. I'm so sorry for your loss."

Debra didn't have any makeup on and dark circles marred the skin beneath her eyes. Her hair had been caught in a messy up-do behind her head with a clip. She grasped Peyton's hand and she held on for a moment, her eyes searching Peyton's face. Peyton opened the half-door and motioned her inside.

"I was going to call you again this morning. My partner and I had planned to come out and see you today."

"I got your message, so I thought I'd just stop by." Debra moved into the precinct.

Peyton usually would have brought her into the conference room, but she had the whiteboard set up with their case notes on it and she didn't want Debra to see she was suspect number one now. "Come back to my desk. Maria, can you get Debra a cup of coffee?"

"Sure." Maria gave Peyton an aggravated look, then she smiled at the other woman. "How do you take your coffee?"

"Black, please."

As Maria bustled off, Peyton motioned Debra to follow her back toward her desk. She grabbed an extra chair from one of the other desks and pulled it up beside her own. "Please have a seat," she told her.

Debra sat, pulling a large handbag onto her lap and clasping both hands around the handle. Her hands shook and she sat ramrod straight as if she was afraid to relax. She was sure in a lot worse shape than Gerald Stevens had been when they talked with him.

Peyton took out her notepad as Maria brought the coffee to Debra and set it beside her on the desk.

"Thank you," Debra said, forcing a slight smile for Maria's benefit.

"No problem," said Maria, but she paused to give Peyton a glare before she hurried back to her post.

Peyton ignored the look and opened her notepad, writing Debra's name on a clean page. "Again, I'm so sorry for your loss, Debra."

"Deb, that's what Darla called me."

"Deb, okay. Do you mind if I take notes?"

"Fine." She looked around. "The receptionist said two of you were working the case."

"Right. Me and my partner, Inspector D'Angelo. He'll be in shortly."

"You're homicide detectives?"

"Right."

"That's all you do."

"It is."

She nodded, staring at Peyton intently.

"Can I ask you a few questions?" asked Peyton.

"That's why I'm here, Inspector."

"Right. So, can you tell me where you live?"

"Westborough." She rattled off an address and Peyton wrote it down.

"Are you married?"

"Yes, my husband works for American Airlines."

"I see. What does he do?"

"He's an Aviation Maintenance Technician."

"He repairs planes?"

"Right."

"And do you have kids?"

"Two daughters – three and five. The five-year-old just started kindergarten."

"Two daughters – three and five. The five-year-old

just started kindergarten."

"Okay. Gerald said you had three kids."

"I'm not surprised. Gerald's an ass."

"Do you work, Deb?"

"No, not while the girls are still so young." Another thing Gerald had gotten wrong.

"Daycare alone would take most of your paycheck, right?"

"No offense, Inspector Brooks, but I'm here to find out what you're doing about my sister's..." Her voice choked off. She drew a deep breath. "...my sister's murder, not answer questions about my family and my work habits."

"I understand that, Deb."

"None of this has anything to do with Darla. I want to know what you're doing to find out who killed her..." She stopped abruptly and her face went blank. "Am I a suspect, Inspector Brooks?"

Peyton set down her pen. "We have to approach every angle, Deb."

"Am I a suspect?"

"Yes."

When Deb's eyes widened, Peyton held up her hand.

"All that means is we need to find out where you were when Darla was killed. You have to understand, Deb. You were the only person named in her will. You're the only person inheriting her estate."

"And that makes me a suspect? Is Gerald a suspect because he should be. That bastard did everything he could to keep Darla and me apart. He never liked me and if he told you that Darla left me everything, it's because she didn't want him to get..."

"Gerald has an alibi, Deb."

Debra deflated, slumping in the chair. She stared at her hands where they clasped her bag.

Peyton wheeled her chair closer to the woman. "I know how hard this is."

"Really, Inspector Brooks? You know how hard this is?"

"Yes," said Peyton, nodding. "My father was murdered."

Debra's eyes whipped to Peyton's face and she covered her mouth with her hand. "Oh, God, I'm so sorry, Inspector. I didn't know."

"Of course you didn't." She held out her empty hand. "Look, Deb, we start with what we know and cross things off as we get more information. That's all I have to do here. I need to make sure those closest to her had nothing to do with her death before I can cast my net out wider."

Debra nodded, reaching for her coffee. Her hand shook so bad, Peyton worried she might splash it on herself, but she got it to her mouth and took a sip. After she set it down, she nodded at Peyton's notepad. "I was at my daughters' dance class that afternoon. They both take dance. The little one goes from 3:00 to 4:00 and the older one from 4:00 to 5:00. We didn't get home until 5:30 because I stopped for burgers." She opened her bag and rummaged around inside, then pulled out a receipt from the local fast food restaurant and laid it on the desk before Peyton. "Here's the receipt for the burgers."

"Can anyone vouch for you at the dance studio?"

"Yeah, some of the other mothers wait with me. They can tell you I never left the building."

Peyton passed the notepad over to her. "Please write their names and numbers down. I have to verify everything."

Debra nodded and wrote the information for Peyton. Finally, she passed the pad back to her, shaking her head. "I can't believe she's gone. I just can't get my head around it."

"I know. Did you know her boyfriend David?"

Debra made a scoffing sound. "Yeah, I met him once. The guy was obviously married, but Darla wouldn't believe me. She was the worst judge of men. Her whole life, she always picked the wrong guy." Debra sat forward. "You don't think he did it, do you?"

"He has a pretty solid alibi. He was on a plane that afternoon."

Debra nodded.

"How did Darla get along with the other agents?"

"What do you mean?"

"I mean did she have any rivalries? These women are all selling these ridiculously expensive houses. Did Darla ever mention any problem with a fellow agent?"

"No, she didn't. I mean, I wondered about it. You know how it can be when people are in competition over money, but she always said that what benefitted one of them benefitted all of them."

"What does that mean?"

"It means that if she sold a house, another agent would likely get a payday too. They all seemed to work together that way."

"What about disgruntled clients?"

Debra shook her head. "That's another thing entirely. I always worried about her. I mean, she'd go into these mausoleums all by herself and it worried me. Some of the clients were eccentric and some of them were just downright creepy. She'd take them out in her car at all hours to see these places and sometimes, when she had an open house, weird people would stop by."

"I thought her open houses were by invitation only."

"In the last couple of years, but when she first started, she took any listing she could get. That's how she and Gerald built the business."

"Did she mention anyone in particular that worried her?"

"Not that I can think of, but I know she got some strange calls recently. Some guy called and wanted her to show him the Painted Lady. He said something about having cash. Darla didn't buy that for a moment. Who has seven mil in cash?"

Peyton frowned, then she grabbed the folder she'd made for the case and opened it, quickly searching through the messages that Stan had transcribed for her. She found nothing from an unidentified male client.

"Did she mention a name?"

"Um." Debra rubbed her forehead. "She did, but I can't remember what it was. It was a real common name." Her eyes widened and she pulled her phone out of her purse. "She sent me a text. I was in the doctor's office, waiting for an appointment, when she sent it." She scrolled through the text messages. "She was so excited when she got the Painted Lady and there was a lot of interest in it. She knew if she sold it, she'd make more money than she'd ever seen at one time." Debra kept scrolling up through her messages. "She was telling me about all the people who wanted to see it – a young couple from Google and some other people who wanted it for a second home. A seven million dollar second home. She couldn't get over that and then...oh God."

Peyton sat forward. "What?"

Debra looked up and met Peyton's gaze. "She sent me the text just the day before she died."

"The text about the man who said he'd pay cash for the house?"

"Yeah." Debra looked back at her phone. "His name was Harold Truman."

Peyton wrote it down, but she knew there was nothing in the messages about Harold Truman. Maybe he was on the contacts list. She rifled through the papers and pulled up Darla's client list, scanning down it with her finger. Tanner, Thompson, Turner. No Truman. Something niggled in the back of her mind and she tried to pull the thought to the foreground. Something bothered her about the name, something triggered an idea, but it was just out of reach.

"Hey," came a voice and Peyton looked up into Marco's blue eyes. The thought slipped away.

"Hey," she said, glancing down at the bags he held in his hand. She could already smell the bacon. "This is Debra Lawrence, Darla's sister, and this is my partner Inspector D'Angelo."

They shook hands, then Marco motioned toward the break room. "I'll just go stash this in there," he said, lifting the bags.

"I'll be right in," Peyton answered, then looked back at Debra. "He brought us breakfast."

Debra nodded, shifting in her chair to watch Marco as he walked to the break room. Once he disappeared, she looked back at Peyton, her eyes widening. "That's your partner? You get to look at that all day, everyday?"

"Yep." She knew exactly what Debra meant. Marco had that effect on women.

"You are one lucky lady," she told Peyton, fanning herself.

"Yep," Peyton said and smiled.

*　　*　　*

Peyton saw Debra out and promised her she'd let her know as soon as they got any leads. Something was tickling the back of Peyton's mind as she made her way into the break room to have breakfast with Marco.

He pushed a take-out box toward her. "It's getting cold."

She sat down and opened the lid, then reached over and grabbed a plastic fork from the cup they kept in the center of the table. He'd gotten her an omelet with bacon and avocado. She felt a little flush of pleasure at the sight of it. They made due with bagels or toast and coffee most of the time, but today, he'd insisted they needed more sustenance. He shoved a coffee cup over to her and Peyton lifted it, taking a sip. Mocha. Another shiver of pleasure raced through her. He knew her so well.

"Debra Lawrence thought you were hot."

He made a non-committal grunt. He heard it so often, it didn't register with him. "She give you anything?"

"Yeah." Peyton cut into the omelet. "She said Darla texted her about a guy who wanted to see the Painted Lady.

Darla thought it was strange because he wanted to pay in cash."

"So? Some people have that kinda dough. I mean, it's not people you or I know, but some people have it."

"Seven million, Marco? Seven million?"

"Maybe he was one of those bubblegum millionaires, Brooks."

"He'd be a bubblegum sevenaire, D'Angelo."

Marco held up a hand and went back to eating.

"The thing is this Harold Truman wasn't on the client list and Stan didn't transcribe a message from him. How did he contact Darla?"

"Maybe he contacted her through January."

"Could be or maybe Stan missed a message?"

"Not likely."

"Maybe I missed a file on Darla's computer. We should have just confiscated the entire thing."

Marco lifted his own coffee and drank, tossing his fork into the empty container. "Okay, so you wanna go back out to Stevens' office."

"I think we need to split forces. You go back to Stevens' office and charm the pants off January. See if she took any messages for Darla and get the laptop."

"And what are you going to do?" he asked.

"Charm Stan. See if I can find out if there were messages he and Maria didn't transcribe."

"You're going to call Stan's tech savvy into question?"

She sighed, reaching for her mocha. "Yeah."

Marco laughed. "Man, I don't wanna be you, Brooks."

*   *   *

Peyton slipped out to the coffee shop across the street and bought Stan a pastry, which she intended to use as a peace offering. She wasn't sure what he liked, but she figured everyone liked cinnamon rolls, right? She sure did.

Carrying it back in its plastic container, she entered the precinct, hoping Maria wasn't at her desk.

She was.

"My God, Brooks, are you kidding me?" she scolded when she saw what Peyton carried.

"It's not for me," she said, then cursed herself for being baited into defending herself. If she wanted to eat all the cinnamon rolls in the City, she would. "Besides, it's none of your business."

"Brooks!" came Defino's voice from inside her office.

Peyton closed her eyes. Whenever she heard that tone, she felt like a little girl being reprimanded by her teacher. She walked to the door and poked her head inside. "Yes, Captain."

"What's going on with the case?" Defino's office was dark and oppressive as usual. Peyton slid into the chair, holding the pastry on her lap.

"We've checked the alibi of every suspect and they've all checked out."

Defino squinted at her, forcing Peyton to play with a hanging piece of plastic on the edge of the pastry container. It made a satisfying twang noise, so she continued. "Doesn't that mean we have no suspects?" said Defino levelly.

"Well..."

"Brooks!"

Peyton twanged the plastic a little harder and a piece shot off, landing on the floor. Her attention focused on it, but she knew better than to lean over to pick it up again. "We're working another angle, Captain. Marco went back out to Darla's office to confiscate her computer."

"Why didn't we do that from the start?"

"I thought I got everything we needed off it. Anyway, this will give him another opportunity to talk to the receptionist."

"And what are you doing?"

"Well, I'm about to run down a lead with Stan." She held up the pastry. "I'm bringing him something to get his brain firing."

Defino eyed the box. "You going to insult his work is what you're going to do and you think that's gonna to smooth things over?"

Peyton scraped her teeth along her bottom lip. Nope. She should have gone to the comic book store. She was slipping. This was the peace offering people brought *her*, not Stan. "It's all I've got."

Before Defino could respond, Nathan Cho and Bill Simons stepped into her office.

"You wanted to see us, Captain," said Cho.

Nathan Cho and Bill Simons were the senior detectives in the precinct. Nate Cho didn't top five six, but he was wiry and smart, and there was something about him that made people take notice, despite his lack of size. Bill Simons was his polar opposite – barrel chested, ham-fisted, and six feet of solid mass. Peyton admired both of them and right now, she was grateful for this interruption.

"Take a seat, gentlemen," said Defino, giving Peyton a pointed stare.

Peyton scrambled out of the chair and stepped between the two of them. "I'll just get back to work."

"Sorry to interrupt," said Simons, patting her on the top of the head like she was a puppy. Peyton would never challenge him because he was built like a house. Besides, she liked Bill Simons. Cho, on the other hand, scared her a little.

"Sorry, Brooks," said Cho. "We can come back."

Peyton backed toward the door. "No, not at all. I've got plenty to do." She stepped outside, closing the door behind her.

Maria tsked. "You better get something on this case, Brooks, or she's gonna hand it over to them."

Peyton started to say something, then thought better of it and hurried off to Stan's lair. Stan was messing on his computers, swiveling back and forth between his many monitors when she arrived. She set the pastry down on the table and pushed it over to him.

He stopped in mid-swivel and stared at it, then lifted his eyes to hers. A smile burst across his face. "Peyton, hi!"

"Hi, Stan."

"Is this for me?"

"Yep," she said. "Actually, I'm gonna be honest, it's a peace offering."

"A peace offering? Why?"

She leaned against the door jamb. "Could you have missed any messages on Darla's phone?"

His face immediately darkened.

Peyton held up a hand. "I know. I know, Stan. It's just Darla's sister said Darla got a strange call from a man who was interested in the Painted Lady. I didn't find any messages in the ones you transcribed that were from a man, except her boyfriend and her ex-husband."

"There were the deleted messages, but those were all from clients who wanted to schedule a time to meet with her."

"Deleted messages? How could you hear deleted messages?"

Stan reached for his own cell phone. "Most people don't know this, but if you scroll down in your voice messages, there's a delete file. When you delete your messages, they go into this file for a few days before they're permanently deleted from your phone. That way, if you made a mistake, you can still find them." He showed Peyton on the phone.

Peyton's eyes widened. "I didn't know that was there."

"Yeah, most people forget about it, or never knew it existed in the first place."

"And you went through those messages?"

"Yeah, I have them saved on my computer too, but there wasn't anything in them, Peyton. It was just people interested in one house or another that she was selling."

"What about one from a Harold Truman?"

Stan frowned. "Definitely don't remember that."

"What about a man who said he wanted to pay cash?"

That got a response. Stan reared away from her. "As a matter of fact," he said, wheeling over to a computer and grabbing the mouse. He clicked away for a few minutes, then he looked up at her. "Listen to this." He punched a button on the keyboard and a man's voice filled the small room. "*Ms. Stevens, I got your number from an ad in the Home section of the Examiner. You recently sold a condo in Gramercy Towers for 1.5 mil. I'm looking for a single family home because I need a garage. I collect vintage cars and I like to work on them, so I need a property that can handle my hobby. You should know, Ms. Stevens, that I'll be paying in cash. I just recently got an inheritance, a significant inheritance, and I'm looking to make a purchase sooner rather than later. I'll text you my number. Please call.*"

Peyton felt a shiver race over her. "Can you get the number off that message?"

"Yeah, I have it."

Peyton grabbed her phone out of her pocket. "Give me the number."

Stan rattled it off and Peyton punched it into her phone. The call rang a few times, then a recording came on the line. "This number is no longer in service. Please check the number and try again."

Peyton lowered the phone. "It's not in service anymore."

"It's probably a burner cell."

"Can you figure out who bought it?"

"I'll reverse the phone number and see." He messed with the computer some more. "It was bought at a Best Buy in San Bruno at the mall."

"I need to know who bought that phone, Stan."

He picked up the phone next to his computer. "Give me some time, Peyton. I'll try to get them to release that information, but I'll need a warrant."

Peyton nodded. "Good work, Stan."

He beamed at her. "I'm sorry I didn't bring those to you as well. I just didn't think it had any bearing on the case."

"You never know what might. That's why we keep pushing," she said. "Let me know as soon as you get anything on the burner cell."

"I will."

She walked back to her desk and slumped into the chair. Now what? She wasn't good at waiting. She needed to be doing something. She wrote Harold Truman's name on her notepad a few times, staring at it. That same itch kept niggling at the back of her mind, but she couldn't pin it down. There was something about the name. Harold Truman. Something familiar.

She thought about what Debra had said, how she worried for Darla when she went to show people houses, how she often showed them houses at night. It seemed like the perfect setup for anyone wanting to attack a woman. A lot of these realtors were women. How did they protect themselves?

She swiveled her chair back and forth, staring at the name. What if Darla wasn't his first kill? What if he'd killed before? Except she didn't remember hearing about women being killed showing houses. They'd know about that. They got information about all the homicides in the City.

Peyton's eyes widened. But what if he hadn't killed anyone else? What if Darla was his first, but what if he'd attacked other women? Maybe they'd gotten away? Maybe they'd fought him off? Her precinct wouldn't hear about those cases because they didn't result in death.

She grabbed her mouse and pulled up the police database, then clicked the search engine.

* * *

Marco set the laptop down in front of Peyton. "January said no one called her about a cash sale. I ran into

Gerald and he said cash buys are rare. They'd have remembered anyone calling to make a cash purchase."

Peyton looked up from her search and blinked at him. She'd been so preoccupied the last few hours, she hadn't heard him approach. "Okay." She scribbled a name down on her growing list.

"What are you doing?"

Swiveling in her chair, she pointed at the screen. "So, Debra mentioned that she worried about Darla when she went out to show a client a house because she was usually alone and sometimes weird people showed up. She also went out at all hours and sometimes put these people in her car."

Marco took a seat in the chair she'd brought over for Debra that morning. "Okay?"

"So I thought about the fact that the killer took a souvenir from Darla's murder."

"The scarf?"

"Right. Either that points to a serial killer or a killer who's escalating."

"I'm with you."

"But we've heard of no other murders with this MO. So I thought, what if he hasn't murdered before? What if he's just attacked women?"

"We wouldn't hear about those unless we knew to look for them."

Peyton pointed her pen at him. "Exactly. So I did a search on attacks in homes that are on the market."

"And?"

"I found nothing."

Marco huffed in frustration and rubbed the back of his neck. "This case is…"

"Hold on." She gave him a cunning smile. "That doesn't mean there aren't reports."

His eyes swung back to her. "What do you mean?"

"I mean that nine times over the last two years, female realtors have reported a man asking to see a house they've had on the market. He contacts them by phone, arranges to meet them at the house, and each time these women have gotten a strange vibe from the guy, like something was off. One woman said he got so close to her, she grabbed her pepper spray. Another said he smelt her hair. And another said she was sure he'd reached out and petted her from behind."

Marco made a disturbed face. "What happened with these complaints?"

"Nothing. Each of them admitted he hadn't hurt them. Even the one who felt like he'd petted her couldn't be sure he'd actually touched her. The cops had nothing to charge him with, nothing to bring him in on for questioning."

"It's not illegal to be creepy, I guess."

"Right, but it gets better. Each woman said he originally got them out to the house because…"

"He said he'd pay in cash."

"Bingo."

"Well, let's go bring Creepy McMillion in."

"That's the problem. I can't get an ID for this guy."

"What do you mean?"

She picked up her pad. "He uses different names all the time. Bill McKinley. Andy Johnson. Jim Monroe. Johnny Tyler. Jim Buchanan. Ben Harrison. Frank Pierce."

Marco's eyes widened. "Hold on. Let me see that."

She passed the list over to him.

"What was the name he used on Darla?"

"Um…" She nodded at the notebook. "It's on the other page."

He flipped back a page. "Harold Truman." He grabbed her pen and wrote it at the bottom of her list, then he studied the list for a moment. Finally, he went to the first name and crossed off *Bill*, writing *William* over it. Then *Andy* became *Andrew* and *Jim* became *James*.

Peyton's eyes widened and everything fell into place. "How the hell did you figure that out?"

"Do you remember when we were looking at Darla's client list in her office? You laughed at a name. Something's been bothering me about that name since you said it."

"Yeah, but I don't remember the name..." Her thoughts clicked into place. "Tom Jefferson. Thomas freakin' Jefferson. They're all presidents."

"They're all presidents," he repeated.

Peyton tapped her index finger on the notepad. "This bastard is using aliases to get into these open houses."

"He's escalating, Brooks. Now that he's killed, he's not going back to sniffing hair."

Peyton shivered. "We need to warn every real estate office in the City, Marco. And we need to call all of these women who filed a report."

"Do you know how many real estate offices there are in this City, Brooks?"

Peyton closed her eyes. They were so not going home tonight.

CHAPTER 8

Mrs. Stevens, this is Angelica Nunes. I just wanted to call you and thank you for your help getting my mother's house sold. You worked so tirelessly for us and it is so much appreciated. I just picked up the check and it's larger than my family expected. You took less commission than you were supposed to. I'm so grateful for everything you did. Mama will be able to afford her care now and that has taken a huge weight off her shoulders. There is nothing I can do to repay your kindness. Bless you!

* * *

Maria laid the stack of papers in front of Peyton. She glanced at them, then up at the entire precinct assembled in the conference room. Sitting next to her, Defino motioned with her hand. "Let's get this circus on the road," she muttered.

Peyton cleared her throat and rolled the dry erase marker over in her hand. "Okay. Thank you all for coming in early this morning."

She had their attention. Marco gave her an encouraging nod. She couldn't believe how much she relied on that single gesture, but she did.

"Last night, Marco and I compiled a list of all the real estate offices, agencies, and single realtors in the San Francisco city limits. We also tracked down contact information for the nine women who have filed a report about our suspect. We need to warn each real estate agency about our perp and we need to interview the nine women. We've divided the tasks, so we can get this done as fast as possible. We're working against the clock." She hesitated and glanced back at the white board with their notes on it. "We think Darla Stevens is his first murder, but it won't be his last.

109

I can't stress this enough. This guy is escalating and I'm afraid someone else is going to wind up dead if we don't get out ahead of this."

They were nodding, even Holmes and Bob Anderson.

She picked up the first set of papers. "Cho and Simons, you'll help D'Angelo and me contact the nine women who filed a complaint. Try to get as much information out of them as you can regarding the encounter. We especially need a description of the perp. This guy goes by aliases. So far, it seems like they're all past presidents' names, but try to find out if he let anything else slip."

"Got it," said Simons.

"The rest of you will take part of the realtor list. Contact the office and warn them about our concerns. Tell them if anyone at all contacts them about wanting to buy a house with cash or gives them a past president's name to contact us immediately. In fact, they should contact us if they feel concerned about a client in the least."

Defino rose to her feet. "Okay, people, grab a list and head out. Let's get this sick bastard today."

Peyton began handing out the lists as people filed up to her at the front of the room. When Stan approached, he paused. "I got the warrant. I'm headed out to the electronics store to see who purchased the burner cell."

"Great, Stan. Let me know as soon as you get anything."

He gave her a tense smile, starting to turn away, but he turned back to face her. "We'll get this guy, Peyton. I promise you."

"I know, Stan. I know we will."

* * *

Marco dropped a sandwich on her desk. Peyton stared at it, then looked up at him, rubbing the back of her neck.

"Thanks," she said.

"Come on. Take a break. You gotta eat something." He jerked his head toward the break room.

Peyton picked up the sandwich and followed him, sinking into the chair at the table and unwrapping his offering. He went to the fridge and pulled it open, staring inside. "What you want?"

"I'll take a root beer if there is one."

He grabbed two cans and walked back to the table, dropping his own sandwich on its surface and placing a can in front of her. She reached for it and popped the top, taking a sip of the bubbly liquid. Then she picked up half the sandwich and took a bite. Ham, her favorite.

He unwrapped his own sandwich. "How many complaints are left to track down?"

"Two. I think one of the women left the area. I can't trace her phone number or her address. She just disappeared off the grid. I even went on social media trying to find her, but nothing."

He took a bite and chewed, considering. "How are Cho and Simons doing?"

"They got through their list and went back to their case. The information's pretty much the same across the board. The guy called, gave them an alias, asked to see whatever house they were representing, offered to pay cash."

He nodded. "Then they met him at the house."

"Yeah, he showed up at the listing some way. None of them remember a car, so no license plate number, not even a partial. Then he walked around the house, not really asking many questions, gave some comment about wanting to see the garage. A couple of the women said he got really aggressive about the garage thing, and that's what triggered a warning in them."

"What do you mean, aggressive?"

"Demanding to see it. At least two of the women broke off the tour at that point. They both said they just had a really bad vibe off him."

"What about a description?"

111

"Five seven, five eight. Stocky. Maybe 250, 300 lbs. Brown, wavy hair. Some said he was clean-shaven, others that he had a five o'clock shadow."

"So, your basic every man," said Marco, reaching for his soda.

"Yep. They didn't remember any distinguishing scars, tattoos, piercings. He wore jeans and a t-shirt. No glasses or physical deformities."

Stan walked through the door, his expression troubled.

"Hey, Stan," said Peyton, setting down her sandwich.

He stopped by the table, shifting weight from foot to foot. "Hey, Peyton."

Peyton could tell just by his demeanor that he didn't have good news for her. "They don't know who bought the phone, do they?"

"Nope. He paid cash."

"Do we even know when he bought the phone?"

Stan nodded. "Two weeks before Darla's death."

She pushed the half-eaten sandwich away. "It's like this guy's a ghost."

"I'm so sorry, Peyton," said Stan miserably. "I'll go back through Darla's laptop and see if I can find anything. Maybe I missed something like I missed the call."

Peyton reached over and laid her hand on his forearm. "You didn't miss anything, Stan. You never do. We're just up against a guy who has planned all of this down to the minute, but he'll mess up. That much I know. He'll mess up and we'll get him."

Stan gave her a worried smile. "But before he kills again?"

Peyton released him and shrugged. "That's the seven-million-dollar question."

He stared at the ground, his shoulders slumping, then he turned for the door. "I'll let you know the minute I get something more," he muttered as he walked from the room.

Peyton braced her forehead with her hand.

"God, that poor bastard has it bad," said Marco, chuckling.

Peyton looked up at him. "What?"

"Seriously, Brooks. The poor damn fool's half in love with you."

"Who?"

Marco shook his head in amusement, continuing to eat. "Stan. He's nuts about you."

Peyton looked away. She didn't want to talk about this with Marco. "What now, Marco? What do we do about this case?"

He finished off his sandwich and then downed the rest of his soda. "We wait, Brooks. That's what we do. That's what we always do." He nodded at her lunch. "Eat some more, then let's go back to the conference room and review all of our notes. Maybe something will jump out at us."

Peyton stared at her sandwich, but her appetite was gone.

*　*　*

Peyton laid her head on her arms, closing her eyes. Her brain was mush, she was so tired. They'd compiled the list of realtors until late last night and then they'd come in early to meet with the rest of the precinct. After they'd made their calls to the nine women who filed complaints, she and Marco had been reviewing notes all afternoon. Dinner had come and gone, and still they had nothing.

She'd drifted into a half-doze when Marco touched her shoulder. "Come on, Brooks. I'll take you home."

She blinked her eyes a few times to clear them. "No, we need to keep going."

"Nothing's going to pop with what we've got. You need sleep. Come on. We'll get back at it tomorrow."

She sat up, realizing she had a crick in her neck from the way she'd been lying. She rolled her shoulders and yawned. God, she was so tired.

He was right. They both needed sleep, then they could hit the case fresh in the morning. After a certain point, they just weren't going to gain any ground until they had time to re-energize.

"Fine, but you pick me up by 6:00 tomorrow. And I want another mocha."

Marco chuckled. "You got it."

As she pushed herself to her feet, Maria stepped into the room. "There's a woman at the counter. She's asking to talk to both of you."

Peyton got an adrenaline kick, her eyes whipping to Marco's face. He gave her a nod, then they walked to the door. The woman waiting on the other side of the counter was in her early thirties, a redhead, pretty, with big green eyes and a curvy figure. She wore a black pencil skirt and a white silk blouse with a red scarf tied around her throat.

Peyton approached the counter, holding out her hand. "I'm Inspector Brooks and this is my partner Inspector D'Angelo."

Marco shook hands with her as well.

"I'm Cathy Anders." She glanced at a slip of paper in her hand. "My broker told me a Bob Anderson called our office this morning."

"Right. He's our CSI," said Peyton.

Cathy nodded. "He gave my boss a warning about a suspect."

"Right." Peyton reached for the half-door and opened it. "Come in and we'll talk."

Cathy moved through the door.

Peyton motioned to the conference room. "Can we get you something to drink?"

"No thank you," Cathy said, entering the room.

Peyton hesitated by Maria's desk. "Tell the captain to come in, will you?"

Maria gave a nod, her eyes following the woman, then she reached for her phone.

Peyton and Marco entered the conference room and took seats across from Cathy. Peyton took out her notepad and reached for the pen in the center of the table. "Cathy, is it okay if I take notes while we talk?"

"Sure." Cathy glanced up as Captain Defino stepped into the room.

The captain offered her hand to Cathy and they shook. "I'm Katherine Defino," she said, releasing her. "I'm the captain in this precinct."

"Nice to meet you."

"Same. Thank you for coming in." She sat down on the other side of Cathy.

Peyton waited for Defino to indicate she could continue, then she gave Cathy a reassuring smile. "So you heard about our suspect this morning?"

"No, I heard about it just an hour ago. I was busy running an open house all day."

"I see." Peyton made a note. "Something about the message must have rang a bell for you."

Cathy nodded. "It did." She jiggled her foot under the table. "I got a message just like the one your guy, Bob Anderson, warned us about."

"Today?"

"No, a week ago." She covered her mouth for a moment and her hand shook.

Peyton touched the hand that lay on the table. "Take your time, Cathy."

"It's just that that could have been me. The woman who was killed. Darcy or something."

"Darla?" said Peyton.

"Right, that could have been me."

"Okay. Take a deep breath." She looked at her partner. "Can you ask Maria to bring her some water?"

Marco rose and went to the door. Cathy closed her eyes and took a few deep breaths, trying to calm herself. When Marco returned and sat down, Peyton patted Cathy's hand again.

"I'm going to ask you questions. Just answer to the best of your ability, then if you remember something I didn't ask, you can add it to your statement. Does that sound okay?"

Cathy nodded, opening her eyes.

"A week ago, a man called you about a listing you have?"

She nodded again.

"What name did he give you?"

"Zach Taylor."

Peyton wrote it on her pad, then crossed off *Zach* and wrote *Zachary*. She showed it to Marco and he gave a chin jerk. "What property was he interested in?"

"A house in Bernal Heights, on Roscoe. Four bedroom on a large lot. Listed at two million."

"Did you arrange a showing for him?"

"I did. That's the thing. I was going to meet him just a week ago. He called and said he was interested in the house. He saw it had a single car garage, but it was on a large lot and he wanted to see if he could extend the garage."

Peyton made a note. The damn garage again. What was this guy's obsession with garages? "Did he tell you anything else?"

Maria entered and set a glass of water on the table before Cathy. Cathy looked up at her as she reached for the glass. "Thank you," she said.

"No problem," answered Maria, walking to the door and disappearing on the other side.

Cathy took a drink, then set the glass down again. She wasn't shaking as badly as she had been. "He said he'd pay in cash. Cash? Two million dollars? I thought I'd hit the lottery. That never happens."

"That's what I gather. It's a good way to make sure no one asks many questions."

"You're right."

"So you didn't meet with him though?"

Cathy gave a little laugh. It wasn't a happy sound. "I got sick. Stomach flu or food poisoning. Puking my guts up."

She stopped herself and gave Marco a wide eyed look, her cheeks heating with embarrassment.

He flashed her his most charming Marco-smile and shrugged. "Happens to the best of us," he said and she laughed, relaxing a little more.

"Anyway, I called and canceled, then we got an offer on the house and the owner wanted to take it, so I called and left a message, telling him I could look for another house." She ran a finger down the outside of the glass and bit her bottom lip. "He never returned my call."

"Do you still have the number he gave you, Cathy?" Peyton asked.

"I moved it to my contacts." She dug her phone out of a small handbag she had slung over her shoulder. She pulled up the contact and slid the phone over to Peyton.

Peyton wrote the number down, then searched back through the folder to find the number that the suspect had given Darla, the one that had been disconnected.

"I could have been Darla. I could have wound up dead."

"But you didn't," said Defino, leaning forward. "And you've given us our first real lead in this case."

Peyton found the disconnected number and compared it to the one Cathy gave them. She looked up at Defino. "It's a different number."

Defino sat still for a moment, then she pushed back her chair. "Will you excuse us for a moment, Ms. Anders?"

"Of course," said Cathy, glancing between the three of them.

Defino motioned Peyton and Marco to follow her, then rose and left the room. Peyton smiled at Cathy. "We'll be right back."

Cathy nodded.

Peyton grabbed the case folder and her notepad, then she and Marco followed Defino over to her office. Defino was already sitting in her desk chair, but she motioned for Marco to shut the door.

Peyton waited until he did so, but she didn't bother to take a seat. As soon as the door clicked into place, she placed the folder on the captain's desk.

"This number might not be disconnected. I'll bet he has an entire fleet of burner cells he uses to contact these women. Once he killed Darla, he disconnected the phone so we wouldn't be able to trace it back to him in anyway, but this one might be operational."

"What exactly are you thinking, Brooks? I can see the wheels turning in that curly head of yours," said Defino with an edge to her voice.

"We set up a sting."

She felt the weight of Marco's eyes on her. "Hold on a minute."

She held up a hand to stop him. "Just hear me out. We get Cathy to call him and arrange a meeting."

"He didn't return her last call."

"But we offer him a property that has a large garage. He's got some weird obsession with garages. We arranged a showing for him and once he shows up, we see what he does. Worse case scenario, he does nothing and we ask him to come to the precinct for questioning. At least we'll have an actual identification and hopefully, an address. Then we can get warrants to search his home."

"You're not sending that woman in to meet with him," said Marco, facing her.

Defino tapped her fingers on her clear glass desk. "Nope, she's not. You're planning to go in for her, aren't you, Brooks?"

"It makes sense, Captain. I'll pretend I'm Cathy's assistant and meet him at the house. Maybe I can get him talking. You can have me wired up."

"He strangled a woman to death," Marco growled.

"Which is why the entire precinct will be outside of the house waiting to crash the party," said Peyton reasonably.

"How about inside the house?" countered Marco.

"I need to get him talking. We need to get him to make a move, something to give us probable cause to bring him in. Part of this will be showing him an actual house. How am I going to explain my six foot four partner lurking in a closet?" She laid a hand on his crossed arms. "I can handle myself, Marco. At least I can until you can get inside. And I'll be in constant communication. You'll hear everything that goes down."

Marco turned to Defino. "Captain, this is too dangerous."

Defino considered, squinting at the two of them. "We don't have anything else, D'Angelo, and Brooks is right. Now that this guy's killed, he's getting ready to open up on the entire City. I can't let that happened."

Marco's jaw clenched, but he didn't argue anymore.

Defino studied Peyton closely. "You're gonna have to look the part. You can't go in there wearing a leather jacket and combat boots."

Peyton made a face. "Then Maria's gonna have to help me."

Defino laughed. "Oh, she's gonna love that."

"First we've got to see if we have a live number. We may be back to square one with this guy if he disconnects the phones after every call."

"And we've got to get Cathy to call him. She'll have to stay here until we see if he calls back. She may not want to put in this much time. You're gonna have to get her cooperation, Brooks."

"I think I can, Captain. She was spooked by what almost happened. I think I can convince her to help me."

"Go talk to her and I'll make a call to our new ADA. I wanna make sure we've got all the legal loopholes closed before we try something this risky."

As she reached for the phone on her desk, Peyton and Marco stepped out into the precinct. Peyton started to walk toward the conference room, but Marco grabbed her arm, spinning her around to face him.

"You're not thinking this through all the way, Brooks," he said. "He's killed a woman and you yourself believe he'll kill again."

She covered his fingers where they gripped her arm. "I know that, Marco."

"And you're gonna put yourself right in his path?"

"With you just outside the house. I'll be fine. I can take care of myself."

"You keep saying that, but Darla Stevens was a lot bigger than you are and she wound up dead."

"Darla Stevens clearly didn't know self-defense. And she didn't have backup. The entire precinct will be there with guns."

"I don't like this. There's gotta be another way. We'll have Stan do a reverse search on the phone number Cathy has and…"

"And what? We know he paid in cash for Darla's phone. He's planned this all out, Marco. The most evidence we have is a partial print on Darla's steering wheel. He uses burner cells and different aliases all the time. We've got a description of an *everyman*, Marco, an *everyman*. We have shit and Darla's still dead. This is our only chance and you know it. We've got to try to catch the guy in the act or at least get enough information for probable cause." She tightened her hold on him. "I don't want another death on my conscience, D'Angelo. Do you?"

Marco looked away, his jaw clenching. "That's low, Brooks, and you know it."

"I know the cavalry will be waiting outside and that's all that matters. Besides, we don't even know if the phone will work or not."

"It'll work," groused Marco. "It'll freaking work."

Peyton backed away from him, ignoring Maria, and headed for the conference room. Cathy glanced up as she entered, her expression pained.

Peyton placed a hand on the woman's shoulder and gave her a smile. "Cathy?"

"Yes?" she asked, looking worried.

"I need you to make a call."

CHAPTER 9

Mrs. Stevens, this is Nora Edwards at the Bay Area Crisis Center. I just wanted to personally call you and thank you for the scholarship you set up. It has meant so much to so many of the women here. Two of our women are starting classes in the fall. You made that possible. Both of them remarked that the future has never looked brighter. That said, I was wondering if you'd be available to come in and give a talk. I mean who better to inspire our women than a woman as successful as you've become. Please call me back, so we can work something out. I'm so excited to have you come speak. I just can't wait to see the women's faces. Okay, well, talk to you soon. Bye.

* * *

The phone rang. Cathy's eyes snapped to Peyton's, the color leaching from her face.

Peyton touched her hand. "Just say exactly what we practiced," Peyton told her. "It's gonna be all right."

Cathy picked up the phone and thumbed it on. "Hello?" she said, then she listened for a moment. "Yes, this is Cathy Anders. Right, Mr. Taylor, thank you for calling me back." She reached for her water and took a sip. "Yes, yes, that's right. I have a single family home on Newman Street in Bernal Heights. It's four bedroom, five baths. Right. Right. It's 1.9 million, but the sellers are motivated, so we might make a deal." She listened some more. They'd spent a long time discussing how to approach this, how important it was to stay natural, normal, even though Cathy was scared to death. "Wait. I thought you were in the market for a house?"

Peyton held up a hand, motioning for Cathy to go easy. Marco shifted restlessly behind her. If they lost him now, she didn't know when they'd get another chance.

"Right. I know the last house got sold before you got a chance to look at it, but you're the first person I've called about this property."

Peyton gave her a thumbs up.

"That's right, Mr. Taylor, you're the first one I've called. I feel bad about what happened the last time, so I'm holding off on scheduling any showings until you've had a chance to see it." She listened, chewing on the edge of her thumbnail in her agitation. "Yes, it does. In fact, it's one of the rare San Francisco properties that has a two-car garage. You know how rare that is."

Peyton shot a look at Marco. What was with the garage?

Marco shrugged.

Cathy waited some more, then she closed her eyes briefly. "Yes, of course, I'd be happy to show it to you. Will tomorrow work? The owners will be out of the house around noon, so I could pick you up..." Cathy paused. Her eyes rose and fixed on Peyton's. "Sure, sure we can meet there. Does noon work for you?" Cathy nodded. "Yes, yes, that's perfect. Noon it is. Do you have a pen handy to take down the address?" She waited, then rattled off the street address for the house where they'd decided to stage the sting. "Yes, that's right. Okay, good, I'll see you at noon tomorrow."

Disconnecting the call, she stared at Peyton without speaking for a moment. Peyton patted her hand. "You did good, Cathy. You did real good." She picked up her own phone and sent off a text to Frank Smith. He was waiting to escort Cathy home as soon as they heard from their perp. "We really appreciate what you've done for us."

"Will you let me know how it goes tomorrow? I really want to know if this guy is off the street."

"Someone will let you know. I promise you."

Cathy gave Peyton an intense stare. "You will be careful, won't you? You don't know how unpredictable this guy might be."

Peyton gave her a smile. "I'll be fine." She glanced over her shoulder at her partner. "I've got a cavalry ready to ride to my rescue."

Frank appeared in the doorway, smoothing down his moustache with a hand. "We ready to go?"

Peyton nodded. "Officer Smith is going to see you home. He'll follow your car and then check out your house before you go inside." She took a card out of her pocket and passed it to Cathy. "Call me if you need anything or if he contacts you again. My direct cell number is on there."

Cathy took it, putting it in the front pocket on her purse. "I will." She rose to her feet and Peyton rose with her. Reaching out, she took Peyton's hand. "Watch yourself, Inspector Brooks. Don't let this bastard hurt anyone else."

Peyton squeezed her fingers. "I won't, Cathy. That I promise."

Cathy nodded, then turned and walked from the room, followed closely by Frank Smith. Peyton shifted to face her partner. "Now for the hard part," she said.

"What's harder than getting a murderer to agree to meet you for a sting?" he asked.

"Getting Maria to help me pick out an outfit," she said.

*   *   *

"That's as good as it's gonna get," said Maria, placing a finishing touch to Peyton's scarf. She stepped back and gave her a critical once-over. The entire precinct was assembled in the front of the building, all except Marco. He was fussing around his desk. Peyton was pretty sure his absence was to show her he didn't approve of what she was doing.

Peyton looked beyond Maria to Defino. The captain leaned on her office door, her arms crossed over her chest. "Can you see the wires, Maria?"

Maria put her hands on her hips and tilted her head. "No, Captain, the wires aren't showing." She grabbed the purse off her desk and rummaged inside. "You need lipstick."

Peyton had found the tan skirt and jacket in the back of her closet. She honestly didn't remember what she'd ever bought it for, but she had it and it still seemed in style. Maria supplied a light pink blouse (a color Peyton would never choose) and a floral scarf. Peyton had no idea how to tie the scarf, so Maria had done the complicated draping. Add a pair of six-inch tan pumps and she felt so unlike herself, she might be able to fool her own mother.

Maria grabbed her chin and smeared lipstick on her lips. "Go like this," she said, smacking her lips together. Peyton tried her best, but she felt like a fool with so many men standing around. She could see the amused expressions on their faces and she wanted to punch someone in the throat.

Handing Peyton the lipstick, she reached up and played with her loose curls, draping them over Peyton's shoulder. "Keep the lipstick. Make sure you freshen it up when you get to the house. And check your teeth."

"Check my teeth?"

"Nothing worse than a novice wearing lipstick on her teeth. Have you never worn lipstick in your life?"

Peyton found her patience slipping. "You're right. I always stop to check my teeth when I'm chasing down a homicidal murderer. It's number one on the to-do list."

She heard some snickers, but her attention shifted to Holmes as he sidled around her, giving her a funny look. "Brooks, you got legs. Who'da thunk it?" He winked at her.

Peyton nearly hurled, but she'd finally found the first person she was going to throat punch. "Bite me, Holmes."

"Okay, wher…" His voice trailed off and his eyes went beyond her.

Peyton turned and saw Marco looming behind them, giving Holmes a death stare. Holmes retreated to a spot behind Cho and Simons.

"It's almost 11:00," said Defino, clapping her hands. "Everyone, move out."

They started for the doors, but Marco caught her arm, turning her to face him. "Put this in your ear, under your hair. That way you can hear us too."

She took the device from him and put it in her ear, then shook her head to distribute her curls. "Can you see it?"

He reached up and pulled a curl forward. "Not now."

She nodded and turned, but he stopped her. "Don't turn your back on this guy for a moment, Brooks."

"I'll be fine," she told him.

"We got a car from impounds for you," said Defino, bringing her a set of keys. "D'Angelo's right. Watch yourself."

Peyton took the keys, rolling them over in her hand. "What did you get me?"

"Brooks!" Defino said and Peyton's eyes snapped to her face.

"I'll be fine, Captain. I promise."

"Good luck," said Defino.

Peyton saluted and walked to the half-door, pushing it open. As she crossed to the outer door, she pressed the button on the key fob and heard a chirp. A cherry red Beemer sat in the parking lot, waiting for her. She gave a little clap of excitement. Marco stopped beside her, shaking his head.

"A Beemer? Suck it, D'Angelo. This is way better than the Charger." She started down the stairs, pressing the button to open the door.

"Nothing's better than the Charger," he groused.

She didn't care. She'd never driven anything this fancy before and she was going to enjoy it.

* * *

Peyton pulled the Beemer into the driveway of the house on Newman. It was a large A-frame, a little out of place in the neighborhood, but it did have a large enough garage to fit two cars. "I tell you, D'Angelo," she said, "I love driving this car."

"Don't get used to it, Brooks," his voice crackled in her ear.

She climbed out of the car and grabbed the purse Maria had lent her. She never carried the things. Purses were always getting women in trouble – they were always fighting to keep the damn things or they were always going back into dangerous environments to retrieve them. Better to keep all pertinent possessions on one's self. She looked out, trying to see where Marco had parked, but the Charger wasn't in view.

Smoothing the skirt, she shut and locked the door, then slung the purse over her shoulder.

"Go in and search the house. Make sure it's empty. Then lock the doors. Force him to knock to get inside," he said as she made her way up the door. He, Cho and Simons had already scoped out the location while she was getting ready with Maria.

"This isn't my first rodeo, D'Angelo," she said.

He didn't respond and she knew that meant he was really worried.

She arrived at the door and found the lockbox on the handle like Cathy had told her it would be. She punched in the code and the box opened, revealing a key. She took the key out and unlocked the door, then stepped inside.

The foyer was dark, so she flipped on the lights. The two sets of stairs greeted her, one leading up and one leading down to the garage, she assumed. She locked the door and set the key on the table by the entrance, then she descended the stairs to the lower level. Except a closet, the only thing down here was a door that led to the garage. She opened it and peered around inside. A few steps down, then a huge open space with tools arranged over a workbench.

She shut the door and climbed the stairs to the foyer, then turned and climbed to the upper story. She went through the rest of the house, finding four bedrooms, each with their own bathroom (a rarity in San Francisco) and a bathroom in the hallway. The decorations were homey – a lot of floral prints, tans and browns, overstuffed furniture. The kitchen looked like a country kitchen from a house in the mid-West, not a major city on the coast – pine cabinets, wooden countertops, a farmhouse sink.

She set her purse on the counter and went to the sliders that opened on the large backyard. Everything about this house seemed out of place for the City. Two car garage, five bathrooms, and a large backyard. No wonder it went for almost two million.

"Is everything secure?" came Marco's voice in her ear.

She smoothed her hands down her sides. She hadn't been nervous at any point in this sting, but his constant warnings were starting to tell on her. "Everything's secure. Is everyone in place?"

"Cho and Simons, in place."

"Holmes, here."

"Smith, at target location."

"Good," said Peyton. "Now we wait." She tugged her phone out of her jacket pocket and glanced at it. 11:45. He wasn't due to arrive until noon.

Going back to the counter, she took out the small mirror and the lipstick Maria had foisted on her, touching up her makeup and to her eternal embarrassment, checking her teeth. She felt like a fool. Even as a little girl she'd much rather play with her father's cop hat than dress in a tutu. It had driven her mother crazy, but she hadn't pushed the issue. All this froufrou stuff annoyed the hell out of Peyton. Wearing a skirt and heels was impractical. The only good thing a dress was for was going dancing, which (come to think of it) she and Abe hadn't done in a long time.

She thought to call him and suggest it, but she knew that would make Marco mad. He could hear everything she said and if she acted like she wasn't taking this situation seriously, he'd call it off but quick.

She wandered around, looking at the bric-a-brac the family had. There wasn't much. She figured the realtor had made them clear a lot of it away, but it always fascinated her what things people chose to put on display. She picked up a tea container. It was a cheery blue color with the word TEA written across the front of it in black paint. The top had a metal clip to hold it in place. She popped the clip and lifted the lid off, sniffing the contents.

She wasn't much of a tea drinker. She didn't see the point. If you wanted caffeine, power slam it with coffee and sugar, lots of sugar. She put the lid back on and lifted the metal clip to secure it, but the clip fell off in her hand. A moment of panic shot through her and she turned the container on its side to see how the clip fit into the lid. She fumbled with it for a few moments, but she couldn't get the clip back in place. Shit, she hoped this wasn't an heirloom or something because she didn't have enough money to replace an heirloom. Not on a cop's salary.

Maybe Marco could figure it out after this was over. Except Marco wasn't any handier than she was. Shit. Shit. Shit. She was just going to have to tell Cathy what she'd done and hope for the best. Maybe they had a bric-a-brac repairman who could replace the clip and she wouldn't have to pay for the entire thing. As she went to set it down, the lid fell off and the container tipped over, spilling the loose leaf onto the counter. Peyton frantically tried to sweep the tea into her hand. No wonder the damn thing had a clip. It didn't want to stay upright.

"Just spotted a guy coming up the street from Andover," came Cho's voice in her ear.

She stilled.

"What kind of car?" asked Marco.

"Walking," replied Cho. "Maybe coming from a bus stop?"

"Maybe. Describe him," said Marco.

"About five nine, five ten, brown hair, wearing jeans and a checked button up shirt. Sneakers. Stocky build, 250, 300 pounds."

"Carrying anything?"

"Nothing, but he's set a brisk pace. He's definitely headed somewhere. In fact, he's looking at the houses, like he's reading addresses."

Peyton felt her heart kick up and her mouth went dry. She hurried to the sink and dumped the loose leaf into it, brushing her hands together to clean them, then she turned on the water, rinsing the tea down the drain.

"Got a visual," came Holmes' voice. "He's definitely looking at the houses. You should be able to see him in about thirty seconds, D'Angelo."

Peyton dragged her teeth across her lower lip, turning off the water. Shit. Now she probably had lipstick on her teeth.

"Yeah, I see him. Brooks, keep the door unlocked after you let him inside. Call out the rooms as you show them to him, so I have an idea of where you are."

"Got it," she said.

"He's turning up the walkway now."

Peyton drew a deep breath and released it, but she still jumped when his knock came at the door. Running her hands over her skirt again, she pushed away from the counter and walked to the stairs, descending. She could see him on the other side, peering into the house.

He looked like any guy you'd meet on the street. Nondescript features, brown hair, brown eyes, a little heavyset, but not grossly overweight. She would never have given him a second look. His hair was neatly combed, his face clean-shaven, and he wore nothing to distinguish him – no glasses, no hat, no tattoos, no piercings.

She pulled open the door, forcing a smile to her face. "Mr. Taylor, right?" She held out her hand.

He frowned at her. "You're not Cathy Anders. I know what Cathy Anders looks like and it's not you."

"No, I'm her assistant. She wanted me to meet with you. She got called away on an emergency, but she didn't want to disappoint you a second time."

He hesitated, not crossing the threshold. Peyton knew she had a narrow window to hook him.

"It really is a lovely house, very unique in San Francisco. I don't think I've ever seen one like it before."

He leaned inside and listened. "Okay, but I'm not happy. She's done this to me twice." His eyes traveled over Peyton and his shoulders relaxed. "What's your name?"

"Peyton," she said. If her smile got any wider, she was going to look manic. God, she hoped she didn't have lipstick on her teeth. "Won't you come inside?"

He stepped across the threshold, but he didn't go any farther. It wasn't a large space and she had to squeeze past him to shut the door. She made sure it wasn't locked. Then she squeezed past him again to motion up the stairs.

"This way," she said and boldly strode up to the top.

He followed her after a moment, looking as skittish as a deer, peering all around as he reached the landing. He didn't say anything, but his eyes swung to her face and lowered down her body again.

"It has four bedrooms, all with their own bathrooms. How many times do you see that in San Francisco?"

He shrugged.

"And a fifth bathroom in the hallway here. Would you like to start with the bedrooms or the kitchen?"

He shrugged again.

Peyton was quickly understanding what women meant by something being off with this guy. He held his hands at his sides and he just stared. Peyton motioned into the hallway. "Let's start with bedrooms."

Walking briskly down the hallway, she came to the first room and pushed open the door. Suddenly she felt him behind her, so close she could feel his breath stirring her hair. She stepped into the room and turned to face him.

"Nice size, right?" she said, too brightly.

"What perfume are you wearing?"

Peyton didn't know how to answer him. "Um, I'm not…I'm not wearing perfume."

He sniffed the air.

Okay, that was beyond strange. She realized she wanted out of this room more than she'd ever wanted anything. Something was just so wrong about this guy.

"I smell flowers." He closed his eyes, sniffing again. "Roses…no."

"Okay, let's look at the next room." She moved past him and hurried into the hall.

He was just a step behind, crowding into her personal space almost immediately. Peyton's hands closed into fists. This guy was begging for an elbow in the gut. She pushed open the second room and motioned for him to go first.

"No, you," he said.

She clenched her jaw and stepped into the room. He crowded up, right behind her. "Here's the second bedroom," she said loudly, so Marco could hear.

"Tell me what the flower is," he said in a low voice.

A shiver raced up her spine. Oh, yeah, this guy gave meaning to the word creepy. "It's probably my shampoo. Um, I can't remember what it is."

He didn't answer, so she turned to face him.

"Maybe you can tell me what you're looking for in a house."

His eyes came into focus on her face. "Let's see the garage."

"The garage?" She realized it came out as a squeak.

"I want to see the garage."

"Why don't we finish up here first? Then we can see the garage."

"Now!" His face twisted.

Peyton squared her shoulders. "Why? Why do you want to see the garage?"

He blinked at her a few times, as if he didn't know what she was asking. Then he gave her a forced, weird smile.

"I have a lot of cars. Vintage cars. I like to work on them. The garage is probably more important than the rest of the house." He stepped closer to her. "Take me to see the garage."

Peyton drew a deep breath. "Okay. It's this way." He didn't move as she motioned back toward the hallway, so she went forward. She hadn't taken many steps before he was right behind her again, nearly treading on her heels.

She turned left at the stairs and walked down to the foyer. Her eyes chanced across the door and she realized the deadbolt had been thrown. When the hell had he done that? She frantically tried to think of a way to unlock it again, but he was breathing on her shoulder, the heat of his body actually radiating into her.

She made a decision and turned to go down the next stairs. She could handle him. Besides, as soon as she got in the garage, she was hitting the garage door opener. No more messing around with this ass.

She opened the door and they stepped out into the vast room with its tools and concrete floor. "Here it is," she said, glancing around as surreptitiously as possible to look for the garage door opener. It should be by the door to the house, but it wasn't.

The slamming of the house door made her jump and whirl to face him. His eyes raked down her body again. He sure gave off a feeling of a rapist, but he'd murdered Darla, not raped her. Maybe he was impotent? Maybe that's why he acted so stalkerish?

"What do you think?" She forced that too bright smile again, scanning the room for the opener.

"What shampoo do you use?"

Peyton's eyes snapped back to him. "Mr. Taylor, I have to ask. Are you interested in the house at all?"

He moved toward her. "I like the garage. The garage is nice."

She nodded, trying to hold her ground.

He sniffed again, closing his eyes. Peyton had an overwhelming urge to run and as she searched the room in growing panic, she spotted the opener near the garage door itself.

"How about I just open the door," she said, starting toward it, "and get some natural light…"

She'd just passed him when she felt him whip around and reach for her. He grabbed the trailing ends of the scarf and yanked, pulling her off balance. The scarf tightened around her neck and her flailing arms accidentally dislodged the ear piece. She saw it skitter away, under the lawnmower.

Grabbing the scarf with her hands, she tried to yank it out of his hold, but he exerted downward pressure, forcing her against his chest. Then he buried his face in her hair and breathed deeply.

Peyton felt panic surge through her and she fought to loosen the scarf as it tightened, cutting off her air. She knew the door was locked, so help wasn't coming and she didn't have long before unconsciousness would arrive. He twisted the scarf around his hand, tightening it, and Peyton gagged. His other arm snaked around her waist, pulling her tight against his body.

Think! she commanded herself. Knowing her window of action was diminishing, she released the hold on the scarf, feeling it dig into her throat, then she reached up and clawed her fingers down his face.

He hissed and his hold lessened, so she raked his face again, then she stamped down as hard as she could with the heel of her pump on his foot. He curled forward in pain and his hand fell away from the scarf. She twisted out of his hold and ripped the scarf away, gasping in air, but she didn't give herself time to recover. Cupping her hands, she slapped them against the sides of his head, directly over his ears. He roared and reared away from her. She didn't stop, grabbing for a shovel hanging on the wall by the door and swinging it. She connected with his shoulder and he dropped to the garage floor, covering his head.

A moment later, the house door was wrenched open and Marco appeared, his gun in hand. Stepping between Peyton and her attacker, he pointed the gun at the man's head. Peyton stepped back a few paces and hit the button to raise the garage door, letting Cho, Simons, Holmes and Smith inside, weapons drawn.

"Brooks, you okay?" said Simons, placing a hand on her shoulder.

She nodded, staring at the man on the ground, his arms wrapped around his head, his body curled into itself. Once he no longer had an advantage, he'd sure gone to ground in a hurry.

Marco moved away from the crowd as Holmes rolled the suspect to his stomach and took out his cuffs. Turning toward her, he replaced his gun in its holster, then reached down and took the shovel out of Peyton's hand. She looked up at him, bracing herself for a dressing down.

"Are you okay?" he asked.

She touched her throat. She figured it was probably bruised, but he hadn't had enough time to do any damage. "I'm fine."

Marco's jaw clenched. "The door was locked."

"I know. He must have locked it after I went up the stairs. I couldn't think of a good way to unlock it."

"Are you sure you're all right?"

She nodded, but the shaking had started. She was afraid to speak or she might betray herself. As if he sensed her turmoil, he stepped forward and pulled her into his arms. She buried her face in his shirt, breathing in the scent of his cologne and realizing she was safe.

CHAPTER 10

Darla, it's Jules. I know this is crazy. I know people would think I need help for doing this, but I just miss you so much. I just wanted to hear your voice, pretend that you're going to get this call and call me back. God, I can't believe you're gone. I can't believe I will never hear from you again. I was thinking about the cruise we took to the Bahamas. My favorite memory was sitting on the deck, sunbathing and watching the ocean. We had Mai Tais and I remember I looked over at you and I said, it doesn't get any better than this. I just want one more moment like that with you. One more perfect spot out of time.

*   *   *

Peyton stood at the window, watching Warren Harding talking to his public defender. She hadn't been sure getting a woman to represent him was a good idea, but Angela Peterson was the only one available.

Warren Harding.

They finally had his real name and whatever record they could pull up. After his arrest, they'd taken him to the hospital to be checked out. Marco had insisted she be checked out as well, then they'd hauled him back to the precinct for questioning, where he'd promptly lawyered up. Turns out, surprise, surprise, that he didn't have millions at his disposal, hence the public defender.

Angela Peterson was looking frustrated as she tried to discuss the situation with Warren. His choice of presidential names for his aliases made a lot more sense now. It was pretty ingenious really. No one had made the connection for a couple of years.

Defino and the hunky ADA Devan Adams strode into the observation room. Devan shook hands with Marco where he leaned against the metal table directly behind

Peyton, then he laid a hand on her shoulder, turning her to face him.

"I heard you got hurt."

She touched the bruise around her neck. She hadn't had time to change out of the skirt and blouse, but she'd ditched the damn scarf. Another reason why she'd never dress froufrou, it gave perps something to strangle you with. Except Devan's eyes were making an appreciative sweep over her. Hm, something to think about.

"I'm fine. Cleared by the doctor in the ER. Just superficial bruising."

"So, what do we have on this guy?" asked Defino.

Marco picked up the folder on the table next to him and glanced over it. "Sealed juvie record. One charge of stalking ten years ago that was dropped when he promised to obey a restraining order. Nothing else."

"Not even a parking ticket?" asked Devan.

"He doesn't own a car," said Marco, snapping the folder shut again.

"Okay, Brooks, you're up," said Defino.

"Um, are you sure she should be interviewing him after he tried to kill her?" Devan looked between her and Marco. He clearly thought Marco should be doing the questioning.

"Brooks can handle it," said Defino.

Devan gave Peyton a searching look.

"I can do it," she said.

"I know this might be hard, but you want to try to get him on your side," said Devan.

Peyton gave him a bewildered look. Was he giving her advice on how to interrogate a perp? "What now?"

"It's always best to build a rapport with a suspect. Make them feel at ease. Then once you have him feeling relaxed, you can go in for the kill. It's a delicate process. I'm not trying to put pressure on you, but all we have is a partial fingerprint. It would be nice to have something more. I know, I know, I've been told this is one of the most difficult parts of this job. However, you're a sharp cop. I think you can handle it. Just stay focused on the mission and it should go all right."

"Well," said Peyton, smiling at him. She could see Marco close his eyes and bow his head. "I'm so glad you took the time to explain this to me. I mean, I was going to go in there, screaming like a hysterical woman, but since you've explained it to me so well..."

"As only a man can," echoed Defino.

Peyton held up a hand to her. "I will just try my hardest to keep my wits about me and not get the vapors." She snatched the file folder Marco held out to her and turned on her heel, stepping out of the observation room door.

"Did I say something wrong?" She heard Devan ask Marco. "I was just trying to give her advice. I mean, that's my job, isn't it? Am I missing something?"

Peyton heard the metal legs of the table protest as Marco straightened and moved toward the two-way glass. "Buckle up, buttercup," he said as Peyton stepped into the interrogation room.

Warren's head snapped up and Angela fell silent. Peyton set the folder on the table and reached for the chair, perpendicular to him. He flinched and pulled away as the chair made a scraping noise across the floor.

Passing the public defender a business card, she settled into the chair, crossing her legs demurely and laying her hand on the file folder. She marked that despite his fear of her, Warren's attention followed her legs.

"I'm Inspector Peyton Brooks. I thought we might talk a little," she told the two of them.

"Go for it." Angela made a motion with her hand. "Ask whatever you want."

Peyton's brows rose at that. What the hell did that mean?

Opening the file, Peyton pretended to peruse it. Then she looked up into Warren's face. "You were arrested for stalking ten years ago, Warren."

"I didn't do anything. I didn't hurt her."

"I know that." Peyton smiled. "That's why they released you, right?"

"Right." He leaned forward a bit and sniffed. Peyton really found that habit distasteful, but she tamped it down.

"I need to talk about Darla Stevens, Warren."

"I don't want to talk about that." He looked away, staring at the cuffs on his wrists.

"Okay, we don't have to talk about that." She smiled. "I'm afraid I wasn't very nice to you earlier."

"You hit me with a shovel."

"Well, that and you asked me a question, a lot. You remember your question?"

"I asked you the scent of your shampoo."

"Right. Lilac. I use lilac scented shampoo. You like the smell of it, don't you?"

He nodded, refusing to look at her.

"You know what I think, I think you didn't mean to hurt Darla. I think you just wanted to be close to her, smell her perfume."

"Lavender. That was hers. Lavender."

"Women haven't been very nice to you, have they, Warren?"

He didn't answer.

"Especially women like Darla. All made up, wearing their fancy suits and heels."

He still didn't answer.

"They didn't even really see you, did they? Unless you promised them money – lots of money." Seven mil to be precise.

"Then they'll listen," he said, but he still didn't look at her. "Then they'll pay attention."

Peyton nodded. "And they try to get away, don't they? I mean you just want to get close, but they flee, don't they, Warren?"

He nodded. "Besides, they shouldn't. They just shouldn't." He gave his head an odd jerk.

Peyton's gaze shifted to the lawyer, who was moving as far away from Warren as she could without making it obvious. She sensed what every woman sensed, that there was something off about this man, something just wrong.

Peyton drew a deep breath, fighting down her own revulsion, then she reached out and tentatively touched Warren's arm. He flinched like she might strike him, then he looked up directly into her eyes.

"They shouldn't what, Warren?" she asked, leaning toward him.

His gaze shifted over her, then focused back on her face. "They shouldn't go out like that."

"Like what?" She tightened her grip just a little.

"Like whores."

"Was Darla a whore? And the other women? Was Cathy Anders a whore?"

He nodded. "Women who work out of the house, selling their bodies. They're all whores."

"Darla didn't sell her body," said Peyton softly.

"She did. She did!" He pulled against the shackles, but Peyton didn't move. Angela actually shifted the chair away from him, though.

"How did Darla sell her body?"

"That was part of it. She showed up in that outfit and acted like she cared, just to draw me in, just to make me say I'd buy, but when I told her I had nothing…" He gave a wheezing laugh. "You should have seen how quickly she changed. She accused me of lying. The whore accused *me* of lying." He leaned back. "She should have known better. Women don't work outside of the house."

"But you go to see these women. You go to the houses where they're working. Why?"

He did a strange thing with his mouth, moving it as if he were talking to someone, then his eyes focused back on Peyton. "What?"

"You call these women and ask to be taken to the houses. If they're whores, why do you put yourself in that situation?"

"They tempt me. They lure me to them with their clothes and their heels and their perfumes, but I know they're whores. I know what sort of women they are."

"Who told you about those women? Who told you about the whores, Warren?"

He stared at her hand on his arm, moving his lips some more.

"Warren, I need your help. I can't figure this out without you."

His eyes snapped up to her face and he nodded.

"Who told you about the working women, Warren?"

"Dad. Dad told me. He told me and Mom."

"He told you a woman who worked outside the house was a whore?"

"You bet he did. He told us both."

"But you still like those women. You still go to the houses to see them."

His shackles rattled as he tried to edge closer to Peyton. "They want me to look at them. That's why they dress like they do, why they wear perfume. They want the attention."

Peyton took a chance. She had no choice. They'd gotten into a circular pattern. "But isn't that going against what Dad told you?"

He nodded, his features twisting. "It's wrong. I know it's wrong, but I can't stop."

"And Darla? Can you tell me about Darla?"

"She didn't want to talk to me as soon as she found out I didn't have money. She went for the door, like you did. I didn't want to hurt her, but I couldn't let her open the door. I couldn't let her go."

"So you grabbed the scarf?"

"And I pulled her back to me. I could smell her perfume. It was lavender. It was really nice."

"And you tightened your hand on the scarf?"

"I just wanted to smell her perfume. I just wanted to see what it was. It was lavender."

"And after you smelled the perfume, what happened?"

He shrugged, staring at her hand on his arm. "She stopped fighting."

"Did you know she was dead? Did you know you killed her?"

He looked up again. "I knew. I knew she was dead."

"And you took her scarf?"

"I took it. I took it because it smelled like her perfume. It smelled like lavender."

Peyton pulled her hand away. "Why did you kill her, Warren? Why did you have to strangle her?"

His face went slack. "She was a whore."

"She was a whore and that made it okay?"

"She shouldn't have been working outside the house."

Peyton straightened. "Why the garage? Why did you kill her in the garage?"

He mouthed the words again. Peyton watched, trying to catch them, but she couldn't.

"Warren, why did you kill Darla in the garage?"

Suddenly Warren surged upward, struggling against his handcuffs. "It's a man's place! It's a man's place!" he growled at Peyton.

Angela scrambled to her feet and pressed herself against the wall. Peyton rose and held out her hands, trying to stop Warren, but before she could do anything, the door flew open and both Smith and Marco burst into the room, grabbing Warren and wrestling him into the chair again.

He spit and sputtered and raged, repeating "It's a man's place!" over and over again.

Peyton edged around him and grabbed Angela's arm, hurrying her from the room. Once they got into the observation room, Peyton watched Warren struggling against the cuffs and the two men who held him down. In the corner, Defino was calling for an EMT to come administer a sedative.

Devan looked over at the shaken Angela and held out his card. She took it automatically.

"Let me guess, you're entering a plea of insanity," he said.

Angela didn't respond, but turned to watch through the two-way glass with Peyton.

*   *   *

Peyton rubbed her hand over her eyes and clicked on another screen. Marco dropped into the chair next to her desk and jerked his chin at her. "How much longer are you going to go at this?"

"Until I have something to give the ADA. I don't think Warren meant to kill Darla."

"But he did kill her, so he needs to be locked up, Brooks."

"Not in a prison. He needs psychiatric help, Marco."

He shook his head. "He tried to strangle you, Brooks. Have you forgotten that?"

She tapped the monitor with her index finger. "Listen to this, D'Angelo. Warren Harding, Senior, flew into a schizophrenic rage one March afternoon and beat his wife to death in the family garage. Fourteen-year-old Warren Harding, Junior, found her body."

Marco shuddered.

"When police asked Harding Senior why he did it, he claimed…"

"It's a man's place," Marco finished.

Peyton gave a weary nod.

"We got him, Brooks. That's all that matters. Now, grab your coat and let's go. We're meeting Abe at *Dave's Dive*."

"Abe's going to *Dave's*?"

"Yep. Look, we solved a case. We get a beer. We can't break with tradition. The report will wait for tomorrow."

Peyton turned off the computer and grabbed her suit jacket off the back of the chair. "You think Defino will let me drive the Beemer for another day."

Marco draped his arm across her shoulders. "I wouldn't count on it. I saw them towing it back to impounds ten minutes ago."

"Damn it," she grumbled.

*　*　*

Dave's Dive was a seedy bar in the SoMa (or South of Market). It had dim lighting, sticky tables that wobbled, and a bar that took up one whole wall of the room. In the past, it would have been filled with cigarette smoke. A pool table stood in the far back by the bathrooms and waitresses in skimpy skirts and *Dave's* t-shirts meandered through the crowd.

Abe had a table secured in the middle of the room and he waved them over. He wore matching set of orange pants and a collared shirt with (God help him) orange loafers. Peyton had a mental image of the store where Abe bought all his clothes and it made her smile, easing some of the tension from the case.

He stood and grabbed her hand, forcing her to twirl before him. "You are delectable, sweets!" he shouted above the jukebox, then his attention focused on her throat. "But what's with the bruise?"

"Hazards of the job," she said, sliding into the cop's seat where she could watch the entire room.

Marco gave her an arch look and she knew he wanted this seat, but she was feeling edgy, so she got it tonight. He sank into a chair next to her.

Abe leaned over. "What'll be your poison?"

"Beer in a bottle," she said, looking around. "I don't want to get hepatitis. Why'd you pick this place, Marco?"

"After every solved case, we get a beer. I thought we might expand our locations," he answered. "I'll have a beer too, but get me one on tap. I'll live dangerously."

"Yes, you will," said Abe in a sultry voice as he went to the bar.

Marco looked over at Peyton. "Stop worrying. Let it go for now."

"I know, and I know that guy needs to be off the streets, but they'll destroy him in prison and I hate that."

"Brooks..." He stopped as a tall man in a perfectly pressed suit appeared at the table.

Peyton felt a flush of pleasure as Devan Adams smiled down at them. "What are you doing here?" she asked.

"I heard D'Angelo tell Maria where you were going. I was meeting with Captain Defino at the time, so I thought I'd see if I could crash the party."

"Crash is right," grumbled Marco.

Peyton nudged him with her elbow. "Of course, sit down," she said, motioning with her other hand to a chair.

He pulled it out, but Abe was suddenly at his shoulder. "Well, well, well, how are you, hot stuff?"

Devan gave Abe a startled look, but Peyton intervened. "This is Devan Adams, the new ADA." She put emphasis on his title.

"Howdy do!" said Abe, thrusting out his hand. "I'm Abraham Jefferson, Medical Examiner, fashion designer, and single." He put emphasis on his marital status.

"Nice to meet you," said Devan, shaking his hand.

"What would you like to drink, darlin'?" said Abe.

"I'll take a vodka martini, neat. And by the way, I'm straight."

"Vodka martini it is," said Abe, then he focused his attention to Marco. "He's not as gorgeous as you anyway, Angel."

"Thanks," said Marco with a tight smile.

Peyton laughed.

"Help me get the drinks, Angel'D," said Abe, jerking his chin toward the bar.

Marco grumbled something, but he climbed out of his chair and followed Abe to the bar, while Devan sank into the chair across from Peyton. He gave her a smile, then leaned close.

"I owe you an apology."

"For what?" she said.

"I questioned your ability and I shouldn't have done that." He tilted his head, giving her an appraising look. "You're a talented interrogator, Inspector Brooks."

"Thank you, sir. It's one of the things I do well."

A slow smile curled his lips. "Is it now? I wonder what the others are."

"You'll just have to find out for yourself," she said, bracing her chin on her hand. Was she really flirting with this guy? She knew what Marco would say. You never date anyone at work. Well, it wasn't as if he was really interested in her.

"I'll never doubt you again," he said.

She pressed her index finger into a divot in the table, deciding she might not have a better opportunity to make a case for Warren Harding. "You know Mr. Harding doesn't belong in prison, right?"

"He murdered a woman, Peyton. He attacked a police officer."

"He's mentally ill. I found articles about his father. He murdered his wife and Mr. Harding found the body."

Devan leaned back in his chair. "I thought this outing was to forget the case for a while."

"It is. I just saw an opportunity and I took it."

He smiled that slow smile again, making Peyton's heart do a little flutter. "Well, what if I see a different sort of opportunity…" he began, but Abe suddenly loomed behind him.

"One vodka martini neat," he boomed and set the drink in front of him.

Marco slipped into the chair next to her and passed her a bottle of beer, setting down his own mug. Abe had something pink in a martini glass, the top of which looked like cotton candy.

"What is that?" asked Peyton.

"A magic mojito. Rum, bitters, lime, mint and of course, the pièce de résistance, cotton candy. Want a sip?"

"No," she said, recoiling.

Devan frowned at his own drink, then he reached for the swizzle stick and lifted it out, staring at the trio of pearl onions affixed to it. "I didn't ask for onions," he said, frowning at them.

"Oh, I'm so sorry," said Abe, taking a seat. "Angel thought you'd love them."

Marco gave Devan a wicked grin.

Devan saluted him with the onions, then popped the whole thing in his mouth, chewing vigorously. When he finished, he turned to Peyton and offered her a wink.

Peyton couldn't help it. She started laughing.

THE END

Now that you've finished, visit ML Hamilton at her website: authormlhamilton.net and sign up for her newsletter. Receive free offers and discounts once you sign up!

The Complete *Peyton Brooks' Mysteries* Collection:
Murder in the Painted Lady, Volume 0
Murder on Potrero Hill Volume 1
Murder in the Tenderloin Volume 2
Murder on Russian Hill Volume 3
Murder on Alcatraz Volume 4
Murder in Chinatown Volume 5
Murder in the Presidio Volume 6
Murder on Treasure Island Volume 7

Peyton Brooks FBI Collection:
Zombies in the Delta Volume 1
Mermaids in the Pacific Volume 2
Werewolves in London Volume 3
Vampires in Hollywood Volume 4
Mayan Gods in the Yucatan Volume 5

Zion Sawyer Cozy Mystery Collection:
Cappuccino Volume 1

The Avery Nolan Adventure Collection:
Swift as a Shadow Volume 1
Short as Any Dream Volume 2
Brief as Lightning Volume 3
Momentary as a Sound Volume 4

The Complete *World of Samar* Collection:
The Talisman of Eldon Emerald Volume 1
The Heirs of Eldon Volume 2
The Star of Eldon Volume 3
The Spirit of Eldon Volume 4
The Sanctuary of Eldon Volume 5

ML Hamilton

Stand Alone Novels:

Ravensong
Serenity

CPSIA information can be obtained
at www.ICGtesting.com
Printed in the USA
FSHW01n2311280518
48766FS